THE LATEST FROM

HITCHCOCK'S SCOUTING REPORT

—Squeeze plays can be dangerous. Or so a play-boy discovers when he tries to frame a derelict for murder in Richard O. Lewis's "The Nice Young Man."

—Emma Dunbar is sidelined, permanently, in Theodore Mathieson's "The Compleat Secretary."

—Nick Farrel gets to first base, but not much farther, the night he meets Anna in David A. Heller's "The Second Thief."

—Arthur Harper strikes out in a big way in Ed Lacy's "Who Will Miss Arthur?"

And, of course, there's more. It all adds up to a grand-slam evening of terror as Hitchcock scores again and again . . . in

MURDERERS' ROW

MURDERERS' ROW

Alfred Hitchcock,
Editor

A DELL BOOK

Published by
Dell Publishing Co., Inc.
1 Dag Hammarskjold Plaza
New York, New York 10017

CONTENTS

INTRODUCTION

Alfred Hitchcock

Organ transplants have undoubtedly proved their worth. I wonder, though, if the medical people are aware of all of the possible side effects. A while back, I learned of one that I doubt the doctors expected to occur.

The discovery came when I visited a friend, Osmond-Smythe, who, as a result of a long and dedicated fondness for alcohol, had had a kidney removed and a replacement put in. When I entered his hospital room, I noticed a small, elderly gentleman seated in a corner, saying nothing, simply staring at Osmond-Smythe in a sentimental sort of way. The old man had large, sad eyes, his clothes were out-dated and he wore high-top button shoes. My initial assumption was that he was a poor relation of my friend's.

During the conversation with Osmond-Smythe—which focused primarily on his determination never to touch alcohol again—I noticed that he kept glancing over at the elderly gentleman in the corner. Curiosity overcame me. I asked about the fellow.

"That's Harry's father," Osmond-Smythe told me, speaking *sotto voce*. "Harry died in an accident and I got his kidney."

"I see. And the situation brought you two together."

My friend shook his head. "I don't even know the old geezer. He isn't here to see me. He's visiting Harry's kidney."

Well, why not, I thought. If the old man wanted to say a final farewell to what remained of his son, certainly that small privilege should not be denied him.

The next time I saw Osmond-Smythe—months later—he was coming in from the golf course. And

who should his caddy be but the sad-eyed old gentleman in the high-top button shoes I had seen at the hospital. My curiosity, naturally, was aroused once more.

"It's a rather funny story," Osmond-Smythe told me.
I noticed, however, that he did not laugh. "He follows
me around. Everywhere I go. At the office, he sits in
the anteroom. At home—well, we've given him the
spare room. It's Harry's kidney, you know. He's looking after it, making sure I take good care of it."

"Now," I said, "I understand why he's caddying for
you. It's a convenience."

"Matter of fact, he's the reason why I'm playing
golf," Osmond-Smythe told me. "He wants me to get
the exercise. It's good for Harry's kidney."

Many more months passed before the uncommon
relationship came to my attention again. Word came to
me through a friend of my friend.

"You wouldn't recognize him," our mutual friend
told me, referring to Osmond-Smythe. "Having a permanent shadow is making a nervous wreck out of him.
And the worse he gets, the more the little old man
frets and the closer he stays to him. He has Osmond-
Smythe on massive doses of vitamin E. And he no
longer sleeps in the spare room—he doesn't want to be
that far away. He sleeps on a mat at the foot of Osmond-Smythe's bed."

"The old gentleman seems to be defeating his own
purpose," I commented.

The mutual friend agreed. "The tragedy is, I'm
afraid he's driving Osmond-Smythe back to drink."

The fear was prophetic. Some weeks later when I
entered a restaurant, intending to dine, I suddenly
heard psssting. It appeared to be coming from a large
potted palm. Investigating, I found Osmond-Smythe
there. He was a mere memory of himself. His hair was
snow white. His eyes were sunken.

"Save me!" he whispered frantically. "I've got to
have a drink!"

I suggested that he try the bar.

"Order for me!" he begged. "When the bartender
puts the drink on the bar, signal to me. I'll run in."

His fear, I assumed, was that his elderly nemesis was lurking somewhere nearby. So, out of pity, I followed his instructions. I entered the bar and ordered the drink he had requested. When it was delivered, I raised a hand, signaling to Osmond-Smythe that his salvation was awaiting him.

Osmond-Smythe burst from behind the potted palm. He galloped to the bar. But as he reached for the drink, the little old gentleman abruptly rose up from behind the bar like an avenging devil. Wielding a stout walking stick, he smashed the glass that contained my friend's drink.

Osmond-Smythe shrieked in terror and raced for the exit. The little old man tottered after him—or, rather, the truth to be told, after Harry's kidney.

Almost unbelievably, the story is soon due for a happy ending. Osmond-Smythe is back in the hospital. The little old man is with him. They are waiting. When conditions are right, my friend will have another transplant. Harry's kidney will be removed and allotted to someone else. What they are waiting for is a donor who will supply Osmond-Smythe with a kidney to replace Harry's. The delay is the result of my friend's insistence that the next donor be an orphan.

I cannot promise that the endings to the stories you will find here will all be that happy. Neither will your kidneys be affected. The spine, however, is a different matter. Expect some chilling.

NICE GUY

Richard Deming

We got the case instead of the Robbery Squad, because when somebody gets hurt or killed during a holdup, it's Homicide's baby. The place was a small jewelry store in the eight hundred block of Franklin Avenue. All the shops in that area are small, mostly one- or two-man businesses. The jewelry store was bracketed by a pawnshop on one side of it and a one-man barbershop on the other.

Gilt lettering on the plate-glass window read: *Bruer and Benjamin, Jewelers.* A squad car was parked in front and a muscular young cop in uniform stood on the sidewalk before the shop door. A few bystanders were clustered before the pawnshop and barbershop, but the area in front of the jewelry store had been cleared.

I didn't recognize the cop, but he knew me. He touched his cap, said, "Hi, Sergeant," and moved aside to let me pass.

Inside, the store was long and narrow, with display cases on either side and with only about a six-foot-wide aisle between them. There was another short display case at the rear of the room, with an open door beyond it.

Another uniformed cop, this one of about my vintage, was inside the store. I knew him. He was a twenty-year veteran named Phil Ritter, and also a sergeant.

I said, "Morning, Phil."

He said, "How are you, Sod?" then jerked his thumb toward the rear display case. "Victim's lying back there."

I nodded, then looked at the other occupant of the place, a mousy little man of about sixty who stood nearby with an expression of numbed shock on his face.

"Witness," Ritter said briefly.

I nodded again and continued on back to the rear of the place. There was a space on either side of the rear counter. I walked behind it to look down at the still figure on the floor. The man lay on his left side with his knees drawn up in a fetal position. He was lean and thin-faced, with long sideburns and a hairline mustache which made him resemble the villain of some mid-Victorian melodrama. I guessed he had been in his late forties.

His right arm blocked the view of his chest, but a thin trickle of blood running from beneath the arm indicated that he had a hole in it. There wasn't much blood, suggesting he had died almost instantly.

I came back around the counter and asked Sergeant Ritter, "Doctor look at him?"

"Just enough to verify he was dead. A Dr. Vaughan in the next block. Mr. Bruer here called him." He nodded toward the little man. "He had to go back to his office, but he said you could contact him there if you want. He also said to tell you he didn't move the body."

"Good."

I looked at the little man. He was only about five feet six and weighed possibly a hundred and twenty-five pounds. He had thinning gray hair, wore steel-rimmed glasses and the expression of a frightened rabbit.

I've been accused of intimidating witnesses with my sour manner. This one looked so easily intimidated that I deliberately made my voice as pleasant as possible when I said, "I'm Sergeant Sod Harris of the Homicide Squad. Your name is Bruer?"

"Yes, sir," he said in a shaky voice. "Fred Bruer. I'm one of the partners in the jewelry store."

"He was the other one?" I asked, nodding toward the rear.

"Yes, sir. Andrew Benjamin. This is awful. We've

been business partners for ten years."

"Uh-huh," I said. "I know this has been a shock to you, Mr. Bruer, but we'll do the best we can to get the person who killed your partner. You were here when it happened?"

"Yes, sir. It was me he held up. I was out front here and Andy was back in the workshop. I had just made up our weekly bank deposit—I always go to the bank on Friday morning—and was just drawing the strings of the leather bag I carry the deposit in, when this fellow came in and pulled a gun on me. I guess he must have been watching us for some time and knew our routine. Casing, they call it, don't they?"

"Uh-huh," I said. "What makes you think he had cased you?"

"He seemed to know what was in the bag, because he said, 'I'll take that, mister.' I gave it to him without argument. Then he came behind the counter where I was, emptied the register there into the bag, then went behind the other counter and did the same with that register."

I glanced both ways and saw identical cash registers centered against the walls behind each counter. "Which counter were you behind?" I asked.

He pointed to the one to the right as you faced the door. "I can tell you exactly how much he got, Sergeant."

"Oh?" I said. "How?"

"I have a duplicate deposit slip for the cash and checks that were in the bag, and there was exactly fifty dollars in each register in addition to that. That's the change we start off with in each register, and we hadn't yet had a customer. We'd only been open for business about thirty seconds when the bandit walked in. I always make up the deposit before we unlock the door Friday mornings."

"I see. Well, you can hold the figure for the moment. First, get on with what happened. How'd he happen to shoot your partner?"

"I think he just got rattled. He was backing toward the door with the deposit bag in his hand when Andy suddenly appeared from the back room. Andy didn't

even know a holdup was in progress. I imagine he
came out to take over the front because he knew I
would be leaving for the bank at any minute. But he
opened the workshop door and stepped out so abruptly,
he startled the bandit. The man shot him and fled."

Typical, I thought sourly. It's that kind of skittish-
ness that makes cops regard armed robbers as the most
dangerous of all criminals. They're all potential murderers.

I asked, "What did this jerk look like?"

"He was about forty years old and kind of long and
lanky. I would guess about six feet tall and a hundred
and seventy-five pounds. He had a thin white scar running from the left corner of his mouth clear to the lobe
of his left ear, and he had a large, hairy mole here."
He touched the center of his right cheek. "His complexion was dark, like a gypsy's, he had straight, black,
rather greasy hair and a rather large hooked nose. I
would know him again anywhere."

"I guess you would," I said, surprised by the detail
of the description. Witnesses are seldom so observant.
"How was he dressed?"

"In tan slacks, a tan leather jacket and a tan felt hat
with the brim turned down in front and up in back.
And oh, yes, on the back of the hand he held the gun
in—" He paused to consider, then said with an air of
surprised recollection, "His left hand, now that I think
of it—there was the tattoo of a blue snake coiled
around a red heart."

"You *are* observant," I said, then gave Phil Ritter an
inquiring glance.

"We put the description on the air soon as we got
here," Ritter said. "Mr. Bruer didn't mention the tattoo
or that the bandit was left-handed before, though."

"Better go radio in a supplementary report," I suggested. "Maybe this one will be easier than the run-of-
the-mill. The guy certainly ought to be easy to identify."

I was beginning to feel a lot more enthusiastic about
this case than I had when the lieutenant sent me out on
it. Generally you find almost nothing to work on, but

here we had Fred Bruer's excellent description of the bandit.

According to figures compiled by the FBI, eighty percent of the homicides in the United States are committed by relatives, friends or acquaintances of the victims, which gives you something to work on, but in a typical stickup kill, some trigger-happy punk puts a bullet in a store clerk or customer he never saw before in his life. Most times your only clue is a physical description, usually vague and, if there is more than one witness, maybe contradictory. Also, you can almost bank on it that the killer was smart enough to drop the gun off some bridge into deep water.

While Phil Ritter was outside radioing in the additions to the bandit's description, I asked Bruer if he had noticed what kind of gun the robber used. He said it was a blue steel revolver, but he couldn't judge what caliber because he wasn't very familiar with guns.

I asked him if the bandit had touched anything which might have left fingerprints.

"The two cash registers," Bruer said. "He punched the no-sale button on each."

Ritter came back in, trailed by Art Ward of the crime lab, who was carrying his field kit and a camera.

"Morning, Sod," Ward greeted me. "What sort of gruesome chore do you have for me this time?"

"Behind the rear counter," I said, jerking a thumb that way. "Then dust the two cash registers for prints, with particular attention to the no-sale buttons."

"Sure," Art said.

He set down his field lab kit and carried his camera to the rear of the store. While he was taking pictures of the corpse from various angles, I checked the back room. It was a small workshop for watch and jewelry repairing. Beyond it was a bolted and locked rear door with a key in the inside lock. I unbolted it, unlocked it, pushed open the door and peered out into an alley lined with trash cans behind the various small businesses facing Franklin Avenue.

I wasn't really looking for anything in particular. Over the years I had just gotten in the habit of being thoroughly nosy. I closed the door again and relocked and rebolted it.

Back in the main room I asked Sergeant Ritter if he had turned up any other witnesses from among nearby merchants or clerks before I got there.

"The barber just west of here and the pawnbroker on the other side both think they heard the shot," Ritter said. "As usual, they thought it was just a backfire, and didn't even look outdoors. Nobody came to investigate until our squad car got here, but that brought out a curious crowd. Nobody we talked to but the two I mentioned heard or saw anything, but we didn't go door-to-door. We just talked to people who gathered around."

I said, "While I'm checking out this barber and pawnbroker, how about you hitting all the places on both sides of the street in this block to see if anyone spotted the bandit either arriving or leaving here?"

Ritter shrugged. "Sure, Sod."

I called to Art Ward that I would be back shortly and walked out with Sergeant Ritter. Ritter paused to talk to his young partner for a moment, and I went to the pawnshop next door.

The proprietor, who was alone, was a benign looking man of about seventy named Max Jacobs. He couldn't add anything to what he had already told Phil Ritter except that he placed the time he had heard what he took to be a truck backfire at exactly a minute after nine. He explained that his twenty-year-old nephew, who worked for him, hadn't showed up for work, and the old man kept checking the clock to see how late he was. It was now nearly ten, and the boy still had neither appeared nor phoned in, and his home phone didn't answer.

"What's your nephew's name?" I asked.

"Herman. Herman Jacobs. He's my brother's boy."

"Mr. Bruer next door know him?"

Jacobs looked puzzled. "Of course. Herman's worked for me ever since he got out of high school."

That was a silly tack to take anyway, I realized. The jeweler had described the bandit as around forty, and Jacobs' nephew was only half that age.

"Following the shot, you didn't see or hear anything at all?" I asked. "Like somebody running past your front window, for instance?"

The elderly pawnbroker shook his head. "I wasn't looking that way. When I wasn't watching the clock, I was trying to phone Herman, that good-for-nothing bum."

There didn't seem to be any more I could get out of him. I thanked him and headed for the door.

"How's poor Fred taking it?" he asked to my back.

Pausing, I turned around. "Mr. Bruer, you mean? He's still a bit shaken up."

Jacobs sighed. "Such a nice man. Always doing good for people. Ask anybody in the neighborhood, nobody will tell you a thing against Fred Bruer. A man with a real heart."

"That so?" I said.

"Only thing is, he's such an easy touch. Gives credit to anybody. Now, Mr. Benjamin was another proposition entirely. I don't like to speak ill of the dead, but there was a cold fish."

It intrigued me that he was on a first-name basis with the surviving jewelry-store proprietor, but referred to the deceased younger partner as *Mr. Benjamin*. Perhaps he hadn't known the younger man as long. I decided to ask. "Have you known Mr. Bruer longer than Mr. Benjamin?"

He looked surprised. "No, of course not. They opened for business together next door about ten years back. I met them both the same day."

"But you were on friendlier terms with Mr. Bruer, was that it?"

"Now how did you know that?" he inquired with rather flattering admiration for my deductive ability. "Yes, as a matter of fact. But everybody's a friend of Fred. Nobody liked Mr. Benjamin very much."

"What was the matter with him?" I asked.

"He was a vindictive man. When he had a little spat with somebody, he was never satisfied just to forget it afterward. He had to have his revenge—like his trouble with Amelio Lapaglia, the barber on the other side of the jewelry shop. Last time haircut prices went up,

Mr. Benjamin refused to pay, they had an argument and Amelio threatened to have him arrested. Mr. Benjamin finally paid, but he wasn't content just to stop going there for haircuts after that. He did things like phoning the police that Amelio was overparked, and the health department to complain that he had no lid on his garbage can out back. Actually I think Mr. Benjamin stole the lid, but Amelio got fined for violating the health laws."

I made a face. "One of those. I've had that kind of neighbor."

"I don't think even Fred really liked him, although he was always making excuses for him. I doubt their partnership would have lasted so long if they hadn't been brothers-in-law," he added matter-of-factly.

I gave him a surprised look. "They were brothers-in-law?"

"Sure. Mr. Benjamin is—was married to Fred's baby sister. She's not a baby now, of course. She's about forty, but she's twenty-one years younger than Fred. She was just an infant when their parents died, and he raised her. She's more like a daughter to him than a sister. He never married himself, so Paula and her two kids are all the family he has. He's absolutely crazy about the baby."

"The baby?"

"Paula had another baby just a couple of years ago. She also has a boy around twenty in the army."

The phone at the rear of the pawnshop rang. As Mr. Jacobs went to answer it, I wondered if anyone had bothered to phone the widow that she was a widow.

The pawnbroker lifted the phone and said, "Jacobs' Small Loans." After a pause his voice raised in pitch and he said, "Where are you, and what's your excuse this time?" There was another pause, then, "That's supposed to be an excuse? You get here fast as you can! You hear?"

He slammed down the phone and came back to where I stood near the door. "My nephew," he said in an indignant tone. "He stayed overnight with a friend and overslept, he says. More likely he was in an all-night poker game and just got home. Good for nothing, he'll be, all day."

I made a sympathetic noise, thanked him again and left.

The young cop was still guarding the entrance to the jewelry store when I went by, but the crowd of curious onlookers had thinned considerably. It wouldn't disperse completely until the body was carried away, though, I knew. There are always a few morbid people in every crowd who will hang around forever on the chance of seeing a corpse.

Down near the end of the block on this side of the street I spotted Phil Ritter coming from one shop and entering another. At his apparent rate of progress it looked as though it wouldn't take him long to finish both sides.

Amelio Lapaglia was cutting a man's hair all the time I talked to him. He had been cutting hair when he heard what he assumed was a backfire too, he said. He hadn't noticed the time, but it had to be just after nine, because he had just opened his business and had just started on his first customer.

His customer must have heard the shot too, he said in answer to my question, but neither of them had mentioned it.

"Aroun' here trucks go by all day long," he said. "You hear *bang* like a gun maybe two, three times a day."

He hadn't noticed anyone pass his window immediately after the shot, he said, but then he had been concentrating on cutting hair.

I didn't bother to ask him about his feud with the dead man, because it had no bearing on the case. He certainly hadn't been the bandit.

When I got back to the jewelry store, Art Ward had finished both his picture taking and his dusting of the cash registers. He reported there were no fingerprints on either register good enough to lift, which didn't surprise me.

I told the lab technician he could go, then went back to give the corpse a more detailed examination than I had before. Aside from discovering that the bullet hole was squarely in the center of his chest, I didn't learn anything new from my examination.

Then I asked Bruer for the duplicate of his bank deposit slip. After adding the hundred dollars which had been in the registers to the amount shown on the slip, the sum stolen came to seven hundred and forty dollars in cash and two hundred and thirty-three in checks. The jeweler said this represented a full week's gross receipts.

From Fred Bruer I got the phone number of the doctor who had examined the body and phoned to ask him to mail a report to Dr. Swartz, the coroner's physician. After that I had nothing to do but wait for someone to come for the body and for Phil Ritter to finish.

While waiting I asked Bruer if he had phoned his sister.

He looked startled. "I—I never even thought of it."

"Probably just as well," I said. "The phone isn't a very satisfactory way to break news like this. She should be told personally. I'll handle it for you, if you want. I have to see her anyway."

"You do?" he asked in surprise.

"It's routine in homicide cases to contact the next of kin, even when it's open-and-shut like this one. What's her address?"

He hesitated for a moment before saying, "She lives down on the south side, but she's staying with me in my apartment on North Twentieth at the moment. This is going to hit her awful hard, Sergeant, because she and Andy were having a little squabble. It's terrible to have somebody close to you die when things aren't quite right. You have trouble forgiving yourself for having a fight at that particular time."

"Uh-huh," I said. "I understand." I asked for his address and wrote it in my notebook.

A couple of morgue attendants came for the body before Phil Ritter completed his survey, but he returned only minutes later.

"Nothing," he reported. "Nobody saw the bandit come in here, leave here, or walking or running along the street. If anyone aside from the two next-door neighbors heard the shot, he paid no attention to it and can't remember it."

There was nothing more to be done at the scene of the crime. I dismissed Sergeant Ritter and his partner, and took off myself.

The apartment on North Twentieth was on the first floor of a neat, modern brick building. A slim, attractive brunette of about forty answered the door.

I took off my hat. "Mrs. Benjamin?"

"Yes."

I showed my badge. "Sergeant Sod Harris of the police, ma'am. May I come in?"

She looked startled. "Police? What—" Then she stepped aside and said, "Certainly. Please do."

I moved into a comfortably furnished front room and she closed the door behind me. A plump, pretty little girl about two years old sat in the center of the floor playing with a doll. A red-haired man in his mid-forties, with wide shoulders and a homely but cheerful face, sat on a sofa making himself at home. He had his shoes off, his suitcoat was draped over the back of the sofa, his tie was loosened and his collar was open. A glass with some beer in it and a half-empty bottle of beer sat on the cocktail table before the sofa.

The man rose to his feet. The little girl gave me a sunny smile and said, "Hi, man."

I smiled back. "Hi, honey."

The woman said, "Robert Craig, Sergeant—"

"Harris," I said. "Sod Harris."

Robert Craig held out his hand. He had a firm grip.

"And this is my daughter, Cindy," Mrs. Benjamin said proudly, looking at the child almost with adoration.

I smiled at the little girl again and got a big return smile. I could understand how her uncle would be crazy about her. I was a little crazy about her myself, and I had just met her.

Mrs. Benjamin said, "What can I do for you, Sergeant?"

"I'm afraid I have some bad news, ma'am." I glanced at the child. "Maybe she'd better not hear it."

Paula Benjamin paled. The red-haired man said,

"Let's go see if your other dolls are asleep yet, Cindy."
He scooped up the little girl and carried her from the
room.

Mrs. Benjamin said, "My—it isn't my brother, is it?"

"No," I replied. "Your husband."

Her color returned and I got the curious impression
that she was relieved. "Oh. What happened?"

Her reaction was hardly what Fred Bruer had led
me to expect. She sounded as though she didn't particularly care what had happened. I saw no point in
trying to break it gently, so I let her have it in a lump.

I said, "The jewelry store was held up this morning.
Your brother is unharmed, but the bandit shot your
husband. He's dead."

She blinked, but she didn't turn pale again. She
merely said, "Oh," then lapsed into silence.

Robert Craig came back into the room alone. The
woman looked at him and said, "Andy's dead."

A startled expression crossed the redhead's face,
then he actually smiled. "Well, well," he said. "That
solves the Cindy problem."

Paula Benjamin stared at him. "How can you think
of that now?"

"You expect me to burst into tears?" he asked. He
looked at me. "Sorry if I seem callous, Sergeant, but
Andy Benjamin was hardly a friend of mine. He had
me named corespondent in a divorce suit. What did he
die of?"

"A holdup man shot him," I said and glanced at the
woman.

Her face had turned fire red. "Did you have to an-
nounce that?" she said to Craig. "Sergeant Harris isn't
interested in our personal affairs."

Craig shrugged. "You and your brother! Never let
the neighbors see your dirty linen. Everybody was
going to know after it broke in the papers anyway."

"It won't break in the papers now!" she snapped at
him.

Then her attention was distracted by little Cindy
toddling back into the room, carrying two dolls. Her
mother swept her up into her arms.

"Oh, honey!" she said, kissing her. "You're going to

get to stay with Mommie forever and ever!"

I thought it was a good time to excuse myself. I told both Craig and Mrs. Benjamin it was nice to have met them, traded a final smile with Cindy and left.

By now it was noon. I stopped for lunch, then afterward, instead of checking in at headquarters, I went to the courthouse and looked up the divorce case of *Benjamin vs Benjamin*.

Andrew Benjamin's complaint was on file, but as yet an answer hadn't been filed by Paula Benjamin. The disagreement between the two was more than the "little squabble" Fred Bruer had mentioned, and Andrew Benjamin's reaction had been characteristically vindictive.

The dead man's affidavit was in the usual legal jargon, but what it boiled down to was that he and a private detective had surprised his wife and Robert Craig together in a motel room and had gotten camera evidence. Divorce was asked on the ground of adultery, with no alimony to be paid the defendant, and with a request for sole custody of little Cindy to be granted the father. Benjamin's vindictiveness showed in his further request that the mother be barred from even having visitation rights on the ground that she was of unfit moral character to be trusted in her daughter's presence. As evidence, he alleged previous adulteries with a whole series of unnamed men and charged that Paula was an incurable nymphomaniac.

When I left the courthouse, I sat in my car and brooded for some time. Fred Bruer's remarkable powers of observation took on a different significance in the light of what I had just learned. Maybe his detailed description of the bandit hadn't been from observation after all, but merely from imagination.

I drove back to the ten hundred block of Franklin Avenue. The jewelry store was locked and there was a *Closed* sign on the front door.

I went into the pawnshop. A pale, fat boy of about twenty who looked as though he were suffering from a hangover was waiting on a customer. The elderly Mr. Jacobs glanced out from the back room as I entered, then moved forward to meet me. I waited for him just inside the front door, so that we would be far enough from the other two to avoid being overheard.

I said, "Mr. Jacobs, do you happen to know if the partners next door ever kept a gun around the place?"

He first looked surprised by the question, then his expression became merely thoughtful. "Hmm," he said after ruminating. "Mr. Benjamin it was. Yes, it was a long time ago, but I'm sure it was Mr. Benjamin, not Fred. Right after they opened for business Mr. Benjamin bought a gun from me. To keep in the store in case of robbery, he said. Yes, it was Mr. Benjamin, I'm sure."

"Wouldn't you still have a record?" I asked.

"Of course," he said in a tone of mild exasperation at himself. "It won't even be very far back in the gun book. We don't sell more than a dozen guns a year."

He went behind the counter and took a ledger from beneath it. I moved over to the other side of the counter as he leafed through it. The fat young man, whom I took to be nephew Herman, was examining a diamond ring through a jeweler's loupe for the customer.

Max Jacobs kept running his index finger down a column of names on each page, flipping to the next page and repeating the process. Finally the finger came to a halt.

"Here it is," he said. "September 10, ten years ago. Andrew J. Benjamin, 1726 Eichelberger Street. A .38 caliber Colt revolver, serial number 231840."

I took out my notebook and copied this information down.

"Why did you want to know?" the old man asked curiously.

I gave my standard vague answer. "Just routine."

I thanked him and left before he could ask any more questions. The customer was counting bills as I walked out, and nephew Herman was sealing the ring in a small envelope.

Amateur murderers usually don't know enough to dispose of murder weapons, but just in case, when I got back to headquarters I arranged for a detail to go sift all the trash in the cans in the alley behind the jewelry store. They didn't find anything.

There was nothing more I could do until I got the report on what caliber bullet had killed Andrew Benjamin. I tabled the case until the next day.

The following morning I found on my desk the photographs Art Ward had taken, a preliminary post-mortem report and a memo from the lab that the bullet recovered from the victim's body was a .38 caliber lead slug and was in good enough shape for comparison purposes if I could turn up the gun from which it was fired. There was also a leather bag with a drawstring and an attached note from the local postmaster explaining that it had turned up in a mailbox two blocks from the jewelry store. The bag contained the original of the deposit slip of which I already had the duplicate, two hundred and thirty-three dollars in checks, and no cash.

I had a conference with the lieutenant, then together we went across the street to the third floor of the Municipal Courts Building and had another conference with the circuit attorney. As a result of this conference, all three of us went to see the judge of the Circuit Court for Criminal Causes. When we left there, I had three search warrants in my pocket.

Back in the squad room I tried to phone the Bruer and Benjamin jewelry store, but got no answer. I tried Fred Bruer's apartment number and caught him there. He said he didn't plan to open for business again until after his partner's funeral.

"I want to take another look at your store," I told him. "Can you meet me there?"

"Of course," he said. "Right now?"

"Uh-huh."

He said he would leave at once. As Police Headquarters was closer to the store than his apartment, I arrived first, though. He kept me waiting about five minutes.

After he had unlocked the door and led me inside, I got right to the point. I said, "I want to see the .38 revolver you keep here."

Fred Bruer looked at me with what I suspected was simulated puzzlement. "There's no gun here, Sergeant."

"Your brother-in-law bought one next door right after you opened for business, Mr. Bruer. He told Mr. Jacobs it was for protection against robbers."

"Oh, that," Bruer said with an air of enlightenment. "He took that home with him years ago. I objected to it being around. Guns make me nervous."

I gave him the fishy eye. "Mind if I look?"

"I don't see why it's necessary," he said haughtily. "I told you there's no gun here."

Regretfully I produced the search warrant. He didn't like it, but there was nothing he could do about it. I went over the place thoroughly. There was no gun there.

"I told you he took the gun home," Bruer said in a miffed voice.

"We'll look there if we don't find it at your apartment," I assured him. "We'll try your place first."

"Do you have a search warrant for there, too?" he challenged.

I showed it to him.

I followed his car back to his place. Paula Benjamin and Cindy were no longer there. Bruer said they had returned home last night. I searched the apartment thoroughly, too. There was no gun there.

"Let's take a ride down to your sister's," I suggested. "You can leave your car here and we'll go in mine."

"I suppose you have a warrant for there, too," he said sourly.

"Uh-huh," I admitted.

Paula Benjamin still lived at the same address recorded in the pawnshop gun log, 1726 Eichelberger Street, which is far down in South St. Louis. It was a small frame house of five rooms.

Mrs. Benjamin claimed she knew nothing of any gun her husband had ever owned, and if he had ever brought a revolver home, she had never seen it.

I didn't have to produce my third warrant, because she made no objection to a search. I did just as thorough a job as I had at the other two places. Little

Cindy followed me around and helped me look, but neither of us found the gun. It wasn't there.

Paula Benjamin naturally wanted to know what it was all about. Until then, her brother had shown no such curiosity, which led me to believe he already knew. Belatedly, he now added his demand for enlightenment. I suggested that Cindy be excluded from the discussion.

By now it was pushing noon, so Mrs. Benjamin solved that by taking Cindy to the kitchen and giving the girl her lunch. When she returned to the front room alone, I bluntly explained things to both her and her brother.

After carefully giving Fred Bruer the standard spiel about his constitutional rights, I said, "I reconstruct it this way, Mr. Bruer. You got down to the store early yesterday morning and made out the weekly bank deposit. Only you didn't put any cash in that leather bag; just the deposit slip and the checks. And you didn't put any money in the cash registers. You simply pocketed it. Then you drove two blocks away, dropped the bag into a mailbox, and got back to the store before your brother-in-law arrived for work. I rather suspect you didn't unlock the front door until after you shot him and had hidden the gun, because you wouldn't want to risk having a customer walk in on you. Then you unlocked the door and phoned the police."

Paula Benjamin was staring at me with her mouth open. "You must be crazy," she whispered. "Fred couldn't kill anyone. He's the most softhearted man in the world."

"Particularly about you and Cindy," I agreed. "You would be surprised what tigers softhearted men can turn into when their loved ones are threatened. None of your brother's fellow merchants on Franklin, and probably none of your neighbors around here knew what your husband was trying to do to you, because both of you believe in keeping your troubles secret. But I've read your deceased husband's divorce affidavit, Mrs. Benjamin."

Paula Benjamin blinked. She gazed at her brother for reassurance and he managed a smile.

"You know I wouldn't do anything like that, sis," he said. "The sergeant has simply made a terribly wrong guess." He looked at me challengingly. "Where's the gun I used, Sergeant?"

"Probably in the Mississippi River now," I said. "Unfortunately I didn't tumble soon enough to search for it before you had a chance to get rid of it. We can establish by Max Jacobs' gun log that your brother-in-law purchased such a gun, though."

"And took it home years ago, Sergeant. Or took it somewhere. Maybe he sold it to another pawnshop."

"I doubt that," I said.

"Prove he didn't."

That was the rub. I couldn't. I took him downtown and a team of three of us questioned him for the rest of the day, but we couldn't shake his story. We had him repeat his detailed description of the imaginary bandit a dozen times, and he never varied it by a single detail.

Finally we had to release him. I drove him home, but the next morning I picked him up again and we started the inquisition all over. About noon, he decided he wanted to call a lawyer, and under the new rules stemming from recent Supreme Court decisions, we either had to let him or release him again.

I knew what would happen in the former event. The lawyer would accuse us of harassing his client and would insist we either file a formal charge or leave him alone. We didn't have sufficient evidence to file a formal charge, and if we refused to leave him alone, his lawyer undoubtedly would get a court injunction to make us.

With all the current talk about police brutality, we didn't need any publicity about harassing a sixty-year-old, undersized, widely esteemed small businessman. We let him go.

I'm in the habit of talking over cases which particularly disturb me with my wife. That evening I unloaded all my frustrations about the Andrew Benjamin case on Maggie.

After listening to the whole story, she said, "I don't see why you're so upset, Sod. Why do you want to see the man convicted of murder anyway?"

I stared at her. "Because he's a murderer."

"But according to your own testimony, the dead man was a thoroughgoing beast," Maggie said reasonably. "What he was attempting to do to that innocent little girl just to obtain vengeance on his wife was criminally vindictive. This Fred Bruer, on the other hand, you characterize as a thoroughly nice guy who, in general, devotes his life to helping people, and never before harmed a soul."

"You would make a lousy cop," I said disgustedly. "We don't happen to have two sets of laws, one for nice guys and the other for beasts. Sure, Fred Bruer's a nice guy, but do you suggest we give all nice guys a license to kill?"

After thinking this over, she said reluctantly, "I guess not." She sat musing for a time, then finally said, "If he's really as nice a guy as you say, there's one technique you might try. Why don't you shame him into a confession?"

I started to frown at her, then something suddenly clicked in my mind and the frown came out a grin instead. Getting up from my easy chair, I went over and gave her a solid kiss.

"I take back what I said about you being a lousy cop," I told her. "You're a better cop than I am."

At ten the next morning I phoned Fred Bruer. "I have an apology to make, Mr. Bruer," I said. "We've caught the bandit who killed your brother-in-law."

"You what?"

"He hasn't confessed yet, but we're sure he's the man. Can you come down here to make an identification?"

There was a long silence before he said, "I'll be right there, Sergeant."

As soon as the little jeweler arrived at headquarters, I took him to the showup room. It was already darkened and the stage lights were on. Lieutenant Wilkins was waiting at the microphone at the rear of the room. I led Bruer close to the stage, where we could see the suspects who would come out at close range. When we were situated, Wilkins called for the lineup to be sent in.

Five men, all of similar lanky build, walked out on the stage. All were dressed in tan slacks and tan leather jackets. When they lined up in a row, you could see by the height markers behind them that they were all within an inch, one way or the other, of six feet.

The first one to walk out on stage was exactly six feet tall. He had straight black, greasy-looking hair, a dark complexion and a prominent hooked nose. A thin white scar ran from the left corner of his mouth to his left ear and there was a hairy mole in the center of his right cheek. He stood with hands at his sides, the backs facing us. On the back of the left hand was the tattoo of a blue snake wound around a red heart.

I glanced at Fred Bruer and saw that his eyes were literally bugging out.

"Don't try to pick anyone yet," I said in a low voice. "Wait until you hear all the voices." Then I called back to Wilkins, "Okay, Lieutenant, let's hear them."

Lieutenant Wilkins said over the microphone, "Number one step forward."

The dark man with the hooked nose stepped to the edge of the stage.

Wilkins said, "What is your name?"

"Manuel Flores," the man said sullenly.

"Your age?"

"Forty."

There is a standard set of questions asked all suspects at a showup, designed more to let witnesses hear their voices than for gathering information. But now Lieutenant Wilkins departed from the usual routine.

He said, "Where do you work, Manuel?"

"The Frick Construction Company."

"As what?"

"Just a laborer."

"Are you married, Manuel?"

"Yes."

"Any children?"

"Five."

"Their ages?"

"Maria is thirteen, Manuel, Jr., is ten, Jose is nine, Miguel is six and Consuelo is two."

"Have you ever been arrested before, Manuel?"

"No."

"Ever been in any kind of trouble?"

"No."

"Okay," Lieutenant Wilkins said. "Step back. Number two step forward."

He went through the same routine with the other four men, but I don't think Fred Bruer was even listening. He kept staring at number one.

When the last of the five had performed, and all of them had been led off the stage, Fred Bruer and I left the showup room and went down one flight to Homicide. He sank into a chair and stared up at me. I remained standing.

"Well?" I said.

The jeweler licked his lips. "I can understand why you picked up that first man, Sergeant. He certainly fits the description of the bandit. But he isn't the man, I'm sorry to say."

After gazing at him expressionlessly for a few moments, I gave my head a disbelieving shake. "Your friends along Franklin Avenue and your sister all warned me you were softhearted, Mr. Bruer, but don't be softheaded, too. It's beyond belief that two different men could have such similar appearances, even to that scar, the mole and the tattoo. On top of that, Manuel Flores is left-handed, just like your bandit."

"But he's not the man," he said with a quaver in his voice. "It's just an incredible coincidence."

"Yeah," I said. "So incredible, I don't believe it. You're letting his formerly clean record and his five kids throw you. He has no alibi for the time of the robbery. He told his wife he was going to work that day, but he never showed up. The day after the robbery he paid off a whole flock of bills." I let my voice become sarcastic. "Claims he hit a long-shot horse."

Fred Bruer's voice raised in pitch. "I tell you he really isn't the man!"

"Oh, come off it," I said grumpily. "Are you going to protect a killer just because he has five kids?"

The little jeweler slowly rose to his feet. Drawing himself to his full five feet six, he said with dignity, "Sergeant, I told you that is not the man who shot

Andy. If you insist on bringing him to trial, I will swear on the stand that he is not the man."

After studying him moodily, I shrugged. "I think we can make it stick anyway, Mr. Bruer. Once we net the actual culprit in a case like this, we usually manage to get a confession."

He frowned. "What do you mean by that?"

"Manuel Flores isn't as influential a citizen as you are, Mr. Bruer. He's just a poor, uneducated slob and not even a United States citizen yet. He's a Mexican immigrant who only has his first papers. He doesn't know any lawyers to call. We don't have to handle him with kid gloves, like we did you."

"You mean you intend to beat a confession out of him!" Bruer said, outraged.

"Now, who said anything about that?" I inquired. "We never use the third degree around here. We merely use scientific interrogation techniques."

I took his elbow and steered him to the door. "If you decide to cooperate after all, you can let me know, Mr. Bruer. But I don't think your testimony is essential. I would thank you for coming down, but under the circumstances, I don't think you deserve it."

I ushered him out into the hall, said, "See you around, Mr. Bruer," and walked off and left him.

He was still staring after me when I mounted the stairs leading up from third to fourth.

I found lanky Sam Wiggens in the men's room on fourth. He had removed the wig and false nose and was washing off his makeup, including the snake and heart tattoo.

Sam let out the stained water in the bowl and started to draw more. "How'd it go?" he asked.

I shrugged. "I don't think he suspected anything, but it's too early to guess. We should find out just how soft-hearted he is when I increase the pressure tomorrow."

I let Fred Bruer stew for twenty-four hours and phoned him about eleven the next morning.

"We're not going to need your testimony after all, Mr. Bruer," I said. "Manuel Flores has confessed."

"He didn't do it!" Bruer almost yelled. "You can't do that to an innocent man with five kids!"

"Oh, stop being so softhearted," I told him. "The man's a killer." I hung up on him.

Bruer came into the squad room twenty minutes later. His face was pale but his thin shoulders were proudly squared.

"I want to make a statement, Sergeant," he said in a steady voice. "I wish to confess the murder of my brother-in-law."

I pointed to a chair and he seated himself with his back stiffly erect. After phoning for a stenographer, I waited for the familiar glow of triumph I usually feel when a case is finally in the bag.

It didn't come. Over the years, I have trapped suspects into confessions by playing on their greed, their fear, their vindictiveness and every other base emotion you can think of, but this was the first time I had trapped a murderer through his compassion for others. I could only wonder why I was in this business.

THE BRIDGE IN BRIGANZA

Frank Sisk

Charlie Thayer was here, of course; old Charlie the lawyer, having his first extremely dry one at the far end of the bar, but he was the only customer of the morning until this young fellow breezed in and started talking about killing himself. He wasn't wearing so much as a topcoat and outside the storm was blowing up to blizzard proportions; no hat either, the snow melting in his red hair. What he wore was one of those sloppy slip-on sweaters, green and furry; a checkered sports shirt open at the neck; and a pair of blue jeans sling-shot tight.

As soon as he plants a foot in the place, I ask, "Is that your car in front, the little foreign job?"

"Mine and the financiers'," he says. "A double whiskey."

"Well, they're going to tow it away if you leave it there, Jack," I say. "It's been on the radio since day-break."

"That's about the tenth piece of bad news I've heard since last night, but somehow it doesn't grab me. I need that whiskey, pal."

"What kind?" I notice now that he looks chilled to the bone, kind of purple.

"I don't care. Any kind."

"Scotch, Irish, Canadian, Greek," I say with a wink at Charlie. "You name it, we probably got it."

"Irish, I guess." He's taken a fresh handkerchief from his hip pocket and snapped it open. "Sure. Why the hell not? It fits."

"She's an Irish girl then?" Charlie asks in that soft voice he uses to edge into conversations where half the time he is not wanted.

"Part Irish," the young fellow says, mopping the melting snow from his face and neck with the handkerchief. "Mostly Irish, with a little Canadian French somewhere down the line." Then he realizes he's talking to somebody he's never seen before. "Hey there, Pop. You a practicing mind reader?"

"I'm a battle-scarred veteran of life, that's all," Charlie says.

"Give this gentleman whatever he's drinking," the young fellow says, placing a finiff on the mahogany. "Ever been married, Pop?"

"Permit me to properly introduce myself," the old boy says, knowing he's got a live one. "Charles Kensington Thayer. Charlie, among friends."

"Munson," the young fellow says, shaking hands. "Walt Munson."

"A pleasure, Walt," Charlie says. "And to answer your question: yes, once upon a time, more years ago than I care to remember, I fell prey to the wiles of a lovely lady and was bonded securely in matrimony."

"You still working at it?" the young fellow asks.

"As little as possible," Charlie says. "May I presume to say the same for yourself?"

"You're firing on all eight," the young man says. Then he downs the double Irish the way it's done out west on TV, only he's not exactly an old cowhand and he suddenly becomes the same color as his finiff on the bar. What saves him from turning inside out is the water chaser.

"Cheers," Charlie says, not really noticing. "Now let me hazard a guess, Walt, as to what's eating you. Satan has entered the garden. Correct me if I'm wrong."

Walt takes five deep breaths and gradually turns white again; pale, in fact, and he says, "You're right, Charlie. Another round of the same, pal. But make mine a single this time. You're right all right, Charlie."

"Satan in the form of a man?" Charlie says.

"What else," Walt says.

"In the form of a friend?" Charlie asks. "Of an alleged friend?"

Walt nods his head and his eyes get moist. "Hell, man, we chummed. Elbow buddies. We played together in a three-man combo a few nights a week around. Not for money, just for kicks. I blew the drums and him the licorice. Benny Goodman, third class, but all charm, all leader. And then it has to turn out like this. Jeez! His name is Charlie too."

"I'm not surprised," Charlie says. "It takes me back to Briganza, down Texas way, where something similar happened to me more years ago than I care to remember."

"Briganza?" Walt says as if the name itself sort of shifted the whole scene.

"Yes, Briganza, Walt," Charlie says, motioning for a refill. "Not a big town as towns go. Ever hear of it? You wouldn't forget it."

"No, I don't think so."

Nobody else ever heard of it either, except some of our regular customers. It's not on any map of Texas I've ever looked at, and I've looked at plenty since Charlie first brought the name into some crazy conversation a few years back.

"Picture, if you will," Charlie says dreamily, "a town with a population of twenty thousand thereabouts and an elevation of approximately three hundred feet above sea level. Sketch in a newly married couple who, physically and spiritually, are living at the highest point in this town. Month after blissful month passes and then suddenly a shadow falls athwart the sunlight. The shadow is an alleged friend of—of whom, Walt? Of whom?"

"Of the husband," Walt says quickly, as if he'd been there in person, and he tosses off the Irish in a gulp. It doesn't faze him much this time. "Give my friend Charlie here another drink," he says. "And me, too."

"Obliged, my boy," Charlie says. "Much obliged. And the happy husband, enjoying to the fullest the sweet fruits of matrimony, looks upon his good friend, who is a bachelor, and pities him. He pities him."

"That's it, Charlie," Walt says. "I pitied the poor lonesome devil."

"You invite him home for a home-cooked meal," Charlie says.

"Many times," Walt says.

"Too many times," Charlie says.

"I must've been blind, deaf and dumb," Walt says, tears in his eyes again. "I trusted him and I trusted her. Trusted."

"But the bachelor is a man of great charm," Charlie says. "He can afford to be. He has no commitments. He is free of the little bickering debates that are part and parcel of even the soundest marriage. He is always seen at his best, and when he is tired or bored he retires. He has the means to buy a bouquet for the hostess because he doesn't have to pay for the meat and potatoes. He can pander to her small prejudices because he doesn't have to face them every day of the week . . ."

Walt slaps the bar. "Oh, man, have you ever got it nailed down! You might've been the rugs in our apartment and not have got it better."

Charlie smiles, pleased with himself. "And it transpired last night here, as it did twenty-some years ago in Briganza, that the bachelor stole away from paradise with the bride of his best friend, leaving nothing behind but an irrevocable farewell message on a sheet of that ruled yellow paper so prized by attorneys for the jotting of dubious legalities . . ."

"They didn't write," Walt says sadly. "They phoned from some place in Maryland, on the way to Miami. Charlie, the cur, seems to've got a place in one of the big-hotel bands down there and sees possibilities of Irene being a vocalist. My wife a vocalist? Nutty-nutty."

"Forgive and forget," Charlie says, taking the size sip from his glass that helps you do it.

"I can't," Walt says, and he goes over to the front window, glass in hand, and looks through the slanting snow at his little car, now pretty nearly covered by drifts. "I couldn't sleep all night from the pain of it, and when I climbed into my car a while back, you know what I had in mind? I was going to get myself killed."

"I guess that's the only real way to forget," Charlie says. "What method did you have in mind, Walt?"

Walt still stares out at the snow. "The Broad Street

Bridge method," he says. "You heard the radio all morning warning motorists to keep off it, especially small cars and trailers. High winds up to sixty, sixty-five, apt to blow you off the bridge and down into the river, a hell of a long drop. So that's what I had in mind when I started out this morning—drive onto the Broad Street Bridge and convert myself into a man-size ice cube."

"Have you changed your mind?" Charlie asks. "And I hope not."

Walt turns around slowly, looking a little drunk and a little surprised. "You hope not? That what you said, Pop?"

"Call me Charlie," Charlie says. "And there's nothing wrong with your hearing, Walt. If you still plan to take the plunge, I'd like to buy us a final drink and make you a proposition."

"Yeah?" Walt says. "Like what?"

"Take me along for the ride," Charlie says, his face very serious. "Pour us one for the road," he says to me.

"I've had enough," Walt says. "What kind of rib is this, Pop?"

"No rib at all, Walt," Charlie says. "I simply think you have the solution to my problem and yours. I should have seen it myself a long time ago, many years ago, but you've helped me put it in perspective."

Walt's eyes widened. "Listen, Pop, if you lived with it all these years, you got it made. It's all downhill now."

"It's been all downhill since the day I left Briganza," Charlie says, and he sighs deeply.

"As bad as that, is it?" Walt asks. "Even after all this time?"

"It gets worse every day," Charlie says.

"Oh?" Walt says. "I'll have that drink after all. Don't they have any bridges in Briganza, Charlie?"

"Just one," Charlie says. "It spans a dry gulch. Not very high compared to the Broad Street Bridge, yet a swan dive from its topmost rail can be fatal. As was the case of the husband (his name was Cyril) in the triangular story I've been telling you about. They say he was split open from clavicle to coccyx."

Walt's mouth falls open. *"The husband?* I thought you were the husband, Pop?"

"I am now," Charlie says with another sad sigh. "But then I was the bachelor of ineffable charm. Looking back over the many bitter cups I have drunk, I am sure that Cyril was luckier than he knew."

THICKER THAN WATER

Henry Slesar

Vernon Wedge didn't want to see the old man. Olga, his secretary, gave Blesker a sub-zero reception, but he sat on in the attorney's waiting room. His shoulders were rigid, his crooked fingers interlaced, his chalky face a portrait of stubbornness and determination. Finally, Vernon had to yield.

"Sit down, Mr. Blesker," he said wearily, pointing to the leather chair in his office. "I know why you're here; my phone's been ringing all morning. Four newspapers, a youth worker, even a settlement house. What have you got, anyway, an organization?"

The old man looked befuddled. "Please," he said. "I just come about my boy . . ."

"Yes, I read the newspapers. And I suppose you think your kid's innocent?"

"He is!"

"Naturally. You're his father. Have you talked to him since it happened?"

"I came from the prison this morning. They're not treating him good. He looks skinny."

"He's only been in custody a few days, Mr. Blesker, I doubt if they're starving him. Look," Vernon said testily, "your boy is accused of knifing another kid in the street. That's what happened. You know how many witnesses there are? You know what kind of evidence the district attorney has?"

"I know he's innocent," the old man said. "That's what I know. Benjy's a good, serious boy."

"Sure," Vernon frowned. "They are all good boys, Mr. Blesker, until they start running with a street pack. Then they're something else." He was almost shouting now. "Mr. Blesker, the State will pick an attorney for your son. You don't need me."

"I have money," Blesker whispered. "The family, we all got together. I run a fuel oil business; I'm selling the big truck. I can pay what you ask, Mr. Wedge."

"It's not a question of money—"

"Then, it's a question of what?" The old man was suddenly truculent. "Whether he's guilty or not? You decided that already, Mr. Wedge? From reading the newspapers?"

Vernon couldn't meet the challenge, it was too close to the truth. He *had* prejudged the case from the newspaper stories, and knew from the accounts that this was one client he could live without. His record was too good. What was worse, he had lost his last client to Ossining. Every criminal lawyer is allowed a few adverse verdicts; but two in a row?

"Mr. Blesker," he said miserably, "will you tell me why you came here? Why did you pick me?"

"Because I heard you were good."

"Do you know what happened in my last case?"

Obstinate: "I heard you were good, Mr. Wedge."

"You told every reporter in town that you intended to hire me. That puts me in a very compromising position, you know that? And you, too. Know how it'll look if I turn you down? Like I think your boy is guilty, that the case is hopeless."

"I didn't mean any harm," the old man said fumblingly. "I just wanted to get the best for Benjy." He was getting teary. "Don't turn me down, please, Mr. Wedge."

Vernon knew a lost cause when he saw one; perhaps he had known from the start how this interview would end. His voice softened.

"I didn't say your boy is guilty, Mr. Blesker. All I say is that he's got a bad case. A very bad case."

Motionless, the old man waited.

"All right," Vernon sighed. "I'll think it over."

The police blotter had Benjy Blesker's age down as seventeen. He looked younger. The frightened eyes gave him a look of youthful bewilderment. Vernon wasn't taken in by it; he had seen too many innocent, baby-faced, icy-hearted killers.

The boy's cell was clean, and Benjy himself bore no marks of ill-treatment. He sat on the edge of the bunk and kneaded his hands. When Vernon walked in, he asked him for a cigarette.

Vernon hesitated, then shrugged and offered the pack. "Why not?" he said. "If you're old enough to be here . . ."

Benjy lit up and dropped a tough mask over his boyish features. "You the lawyer my old man hired?"

"That's right. My name is Vernon Wedge."

"When do I get out of here?"

"You don't, not until the trial. They've refused bail."

"When's the trial?"

"Don't rush it," Vernon growled. "We need every minute of delay we can get. Don't think this is going to be easy."

Benjy leaned back, casual. "I didn't cut that guy," he said evenly. "I didn't have anything to do with it."

Vernon grunted, and pulled a sheet of handwritten notes out of his pocket.

"You admitted that you knew Kenny Tarcher?"

"Sure I knew him. We went to Manual Trades together."

"They tell me Kenny was a member of a gang called The Aces. You ever run with them?"

"With that bunch?" Benjy sneered, and blew a column of smoke. "I was a Baron. The Barons don't mix with those bums. You know who they take into that gang? A whole lot of—"

"Never mind," Vernon snapped. "We can talk about your social life later. You were a Baron and Kenny was an Ace, so that made you natural enemies. You had a rumble last month, and this Kenny Tarcher beat up on you pretty good. Don't give me any arguments about this, it's ancient history."

Benjy's mouth was quivering. "Look, Mr. Wedge, we don't have that kind of gang. You know Mr. Knapp—"

"The youth worker? I just came from him."

"He'll tell you about the Barons, Mr. Wedge, we're

not a bunch of hoods. We got a basketball team and everything."

Vernon smothered a smile. "Why do you carry a knife, Benjy?"

"It's no switchblade, Mr. Wedge. It's more like a boy scout knife; I mean, they sell 'em all over. I use it for whittlin' and stuff like that."

"Whittling?" It was hard to hide the sneer. The end of Benjy's cigarette flared, as did his temper.

"Look, whose side are you on? I didn't stick Kenny, somebody else did! I swear I didn't kill him!"

"Take it easy. I'm not making accusations, kid, that's the court's job. Now sit back and relax. I'm going over the story, from the police side, and then you can tell me where they're wrong. Every little thing, understand?"

Benjy swallowed hard. Then he nodded.

"It was ten minutes to midnight on June 21," Vernon said, watching him. "You and two other guys were walking down Thurmond Street; you came out of a movie house. Kenny Tarcher came out of the corner apartment building on Thurmond and Avenue C. You bumped into each other, and there was some horseplay. The next thing that happens, you and your pals start running down the street. Kenny falls down and tries to crawl to the stoop of his house. There were two people on the steps. They saw you running. They saw Kenny die, right in front of them. He had an eight-inch gash in his stomach . . ."

Benjy looked sick.

"Ten minutes later, the cops caught up with you in your old man's fuel supply store on Chester Street. The knife was still in your pocket." He paused.

"I didn't cut him," the boy said grimly. "All the rest of that stuff, that's true. But I don't know who cut Kenny."

"Who were the other two guys with you?"

"I never saw 'em before. I met 'em in the movies."

"Don't give me that!"

"What the hell do you want from me?" Benjy bellowed. "I tell you I don't know those guys! One of them must have done it, I didn't! When I saw he was hurt, I ran. That's all it was!"

"You had the knife—"

"I didn't use it!"

"That knife is Exhibit A," the lawyer said. "You know that, don't you? The witnesses saw you holding it—"

"Leave me alone! You ain't here to help me!"

Vernon got up.

"I am, Benjy. The only way you can be helped, kid. I want you to cop a plea."

"What?"

"I want you to plead guilty. Believe me, it's the only sensible thing to do. You put this case to a jury, I swear you'll be spending the rest of your life in a cage. Plead guilty, and the worst you'll get is twenty years. That's not as bad as it sounds; you'll be eligible for parole in five."

"I won't do it!" Benjy screamed. "I'm innocent! I'm not goin' to jail for something I didn't do!"

"I'm talking sense, kid, why won't you listen?"

"I didn't do it! I didn't!"

Vernon sighed. The corners of his mouth softened, and he dropped a hand on the boy's shoulder.

"Listen," he said gently. "I really want to help you, son."

For a moment, Benjy was still. Then he threw off the arm of sympathy, and snarled at the attorney.

"I'm not your son! I got a father!"

Like father, like son, Vernon thought wryly, looking at the mulish mouth and marble eyes of the old man. He was sure Blesker had a softer side. Under other circumstances, he would smile and tell jokes and hum old-country tunes. Now, faced with the lawyer's blunt advice, he was hard as a rock.

"You've got to talk some sense into him," Vernon said. "He doesn't know what's good for him. If he pleads guilty to murder in the second degree, the judge will be lenient."

"But he goes to prison? For something he didn't do?"

"You're his father, Mr. Blesker. You're ignoring facts."

"The facts are wrong!" Blesker put his fists on his knees and pounded them once. When he looked up again, there was a new mood in his eyes. "You tell me something, Mr. Wedge—"

"Yes?"

"You don't like to lose cases, am I right? That's what they say about you."

"Is that bad?"

"If my boy pleads guilty, you don't lose nothing. You still got your good record, right?"

"Do you think that's my only reason?"

Blesker shrugged. "I'm only asking, Mr. Wedge. I don't know nothing about the law."

Unable to refute this accurate estimate of his inner thoughts, Vernon tried to summon up an angry denial and failed. He shrugged his shoulders.

"All right," he said grudgingly. "So we plead Not Guilty. I'll do everything I can to make it stick."

Blesker examined his face for signs of sincerity. He seemed satisfied.

Vernon came to the courtroom on opening day with a heart as heavy as his brief case. Surprisingly, the first day didn't go badly. Judge Angus Dwight had been assigned to the bench. In spite of his dour look, Vernon knew him to be scrupulously fair and sneakily sentimental. Wickers, the prosecuting attorney, was a golden-haired Adonis with a theatrical delivery, a keen mind, and an appeal for the ladies. Fortunately, the impaneled jurors were men with only two exceptions, and they were women far past the age of coquetry. During the first hour, Wickers' facetiousness in his opening remarks drew a rebuke from the judge concerning the seriousness of the affair; Vernon's hopes lifted a notch.

But it was his only good day. On the second afternoon, Wickers called a man named Sol Dankers to the witness chair.

"Mr. Dankers," he said smoothly, "you were present

at the time of Kenneth Tarcher's slaying, isn't that so?"

"That's right," Dankers said heavily. He was a hard-breathing, bespectacled man with a red-veined nose. "I was sittin' on the stoop, when these kids start foolin' around. Next thing I know, one of 'em's stumbling to the stoop, bleedin' like a pig. He drops dead right at the feet of me and my Mrs. I was an hour gettin' the bloodstains off my shoes."

"Is that all you saw?"

"No, sir. I seen that boy, the one over there, runnin' away with a knife in his hand."

Then it was Vernon's turn.

"Mr. Dankers, is it true your eyesight is impaired?"

"True enough. I'm sixty-two, son, wait 'til you're my age."

He drew a laugh and a rap of the gavel.

"It was almost midnight on a street not particularly well lit. Yet you saw a knife—" he pointed to the table where Exhibit A rested—"that knife, in Benjamin Blesker's hand?"

"It was sort of flashin' in the light, if you know what I mean. But to tell you the truth, I wouldn't have noticed if Mrs. Dankers hadn't said, 'look at that boy, he's got a knife!' "

The crowd buzzed, and Vernon frowned at the inadvertent hearsay testimony. The damage was done; he didn't even bother to voice a complaint.

Mrs. Dankers testified next; there was nothing wrong with *her* eyes, she said stoutly, and she knew a knife when she saw one. It was the third witness who did the most harm. He was Marty Knapp, a dedicated youth worker serving the neighborhood.

"No, Benjy isn't a bad kid," he said thoughtfully. "But he had a temper. And he never forgave Kenny Tarcher for the beating he gave him."

"Then in your opinion," Wickers said triumphantly, "this *might* have been a grudge killing? Not just a sudden scuffle or unplanned assault, but a deliberate, cold-blooded—"

Vernon was on his feet, shouting objections. Judge Dwight took his side at once, but the impression was indelible in the collective mind of the jury. When Vernon sat down again, he felt as forlorn as Benjy Blesker looked.

On the eve of the fourth day, he went to see him.

"What do you say, Benjy?" he said quietly. "You see the way things are going? I'm pulling out the whole bag of tricks, and I'm not fooling anybody."

"Try harder!" Benjy snapped.

"If I knew how to work miracles, I'd work one. Look, this state doesn't like to hang kids, but it's happened before—"

"Hang?" the boy said incredulously. "You're crazy!"

"Even if you got life, know what that means? Even if you got paroled in twenty years, you'll be thirty-seven years old, almost middle-aged, with a record."

There were tears flooding Benjy's eyes. It was the first sign of a crumpling defense, and the lawyer moved in swiftly.

"Plead guilty," he said earnestly. "Plead guilty, Benjy. It's not too late."

The boy's head snapped up.

"No!" he screamed. "I didn't do it!"

The fourth day was the worst of all. Vernon railed mercilessly at the prosecution witnesses. He called Dankers a weak-eyed, boozing liar. He forced Mrs. Dankers to admit that she hated the neighborhood kids, and the Barons especially. He got Knapp, the youth worker, to recite every detail of Benjy's good record. But through it all, the jury shifted restlessly, bored, irritated, obviously unimpressed by the "character" testimony, eager only for facts, the bloodier the better.

Wickers gave them what they wanted. Wickers treated them to a blow-by-blow reenactment of the stabbing. He bled for them. He clutched his stomach. He put the victim's mother on the stand. He let her cry through ten minutes of pointless testimony, until even Judge Dwight got sick of the spectacle. But it was working. Vernon, jury-smart, knew it was working.

The trial was almost over. Wickers, waving the knife under Benjy Blesker's nose, got him to admit that it was his, admit that he was never without it, admit that he had it in his pocket—maybe even in his hand—the night of the slaying. It was his curtain-closer. Wickers sat down, the prosecution's case stated.

One more day, and it would be finished.

There was a weekend hiatus before the trial resumed. Vernon Wedge spent the time thinking.

It was the old man's fault, he thought bitterly. It was old man Blesker who was behind all the trouble. His faith in Benjy was the indomitable, obstinate faith of the fanatic. Even if the boy was guilty, concern for his father would prevent him from admitting the truth.

"The funny thing is," he told Olga, his secretary, "if I was on that jury, I wouldn't know how to vote."

Olga clucked.

"You don't look well," she said. "You look anemic. When this is over, you ought to see a doctor."

"A headshrinker, that's what I ought to see."

"I mean a doctor," Olga said firmly.

It was then that the idea was born. Vernon looked at his secretary queerly, and stood up behind the desk.

"You know, it's a thought. Maybe I ought to see one. You remember Doc Hagerty?"

"No."

"Sure you remember! On the Hofstraw case, 1958—"

"But *he's* not the kind of doctor I mean. I mean a good all-around G.P."

"I'm going out," Vernon said suddenly. "I'll be at the Dugan Hospital if you need me. But don't bother me unless it's urgent."

He found Hagerty in the basement laboratory of the Dugan Hospital. Olga was right: Hagerty was no chest-thumping, tongue-depressing practitioner; he was more biochemist than physician. But he was what Vernon needed.

Hagerty was a white-haired man with shoulders rounded from years of bending over microscopes, and

he smelt vaguely of sulphur. He turned out to be ignorant of the trial. Vernon summarized the facts briefly,
and then talked about blood.

"You mean there were no benzidine tests made?"
Hagerty said quickly. "Of the murder weapon?"

"Yes," Vernon admitted, "and the test proved negative. There weren't any bloodstains on the knife, you
understand, it was clean. The prosecution claims that
all traces were wiped or washed off. It's never been
much of an issue up till now. But I once heard you talk
about a more sensitive test than benzidine—"

"There is," Hagerty grunted. "Benzidine is the standard blood test in this city, but there's another one. It's
a lot more delicate, in my opinion, and it's not always
employed. It's called the reduced phenolphthalein test,
and depending on a couple of factors, it might be just
what you're looking for.

"The quality of the blade metal, for one thing. And
even if the metal is porous enough to retain microscop-
ic particles of blood, it may be impossible to determine *whose*. If your boy ever cut his finger, or somebody else—"

"What do we have to do?" Vernon said excitedly.

"Get me the knife."

"That's impossible. It's court property at the moment."

"Then get me half a dozen like it."

The lawyer spent all of Saturday morning searching
for the weapon's counterpart. His mental picture of it
was sharp; he recalled every curlicue on its handle; he
even remembered the letters at the base of the blade:
B.L. CO. USA.

He finally found one in a dingy variety store four
blocks from the scene of the stabbing. The proprietor
had exactly five left in stock; he took them all.

There was a two-hour wait that afternoon before he
could see Hagerty again; when the white-haired doctor
joined him in the laboratory, he didn't apologize.

"I have the solution all ready," he said crisply. "You
sure this is the same make of knife?"

"Positive."

Hagerty sprung the large blade. Then he removed a bottle of whole blood from a cabinet, and dipped it inside. Vernon swallowed in revulsion as Hagerty wiped the blade clean with a soft cloth, and marked the knife with a pencil.

"Any trace?" he said, offering it for examination.

"Clean as a whistle."

Hagerty brought all five blades to a beaker filled with a murky liquid. Vernon helped him open all the knives, and they were ready for the demonstration.

"Mix 'em up good," Hagerty said. "It's like a magic trick; you shuffle 'em up, I'll find the one."

Vernon scrambled the knives. Then, one by one, Hagerty dipped them into the solution.

The third one turned the liquid pink. It was the knife that had been marked.

"It works," Vernon breathed. "It really works."

"The metal is porous. If there were bloodstains on it from years ago, this test would show it up."

"Thank you," Vernon said humbly. "You've saved my life, Doc."

"*Your* life?" Hagerty said dryly.

When Vernon entered Benjy's cell, the boy was reading a pulp magazine with intense concentration. He seemed detached, disinterested. Vernon understood it; he had seen this before in the condemned.

"Listen to me," he said harshly. "Listen good. I have an idea that might save you, but I have to know the truth."

"I told you everything—"

"There's a test," the lawyer said. "A test that can determine whether or not there was ever blood on that knife of yours."

"So?"

"I propose to make that test in court on Monday. If it's negative, the jury will know you didn't kill Kenny Tarcher."

"I don't understand that kind of stuff—"

"I'm not asking you to understand," Vernon said tautly. "If you stabbed that boy, a solution is going to turn pink and you can kiss your freedom goodbye.

What's more, if you ever cut *anybody* with that knife, even yourself, it'll turn pink. So I want you to tell me now. *Was there ever blood on that knife?*"

"I told you I didn't cut him!"

"You moron!" Vernon shouted. "Do you understand my question? Was there ever blood of *any* kind on that knife?"

"No! It was brand-new. I never cut anybody with it."

"You're sure? Absolutely sure?"

"I told you, didn't I?"

"This is scientific stuff, boy, don't think you can fool a test tube!"

"I said it's clean!"

Vernon Wedge sighed, and stood up.

"Okay, Benjy. We'll see how clean it is. We'll give it a bath. And God help you if you lied to me."

On Monday, Wickers rose to make his final peroration. He was bland-faced, a picture of confidence. Vernon looked at the vacant faces of the jurors, waiting for their emotional rubdown. But he wasn't going to allow it.

He stood up, and addressed Judge Dwight.

"Your Honor, something occurred over the weekend which I consider of paramount importance to this case. I ask the court's permission to introduce new evidence."

"Objection," Wickers said calmly. "The defense has had sufficient time for the introduction of evidence. I suggest this is a delaying tactic."

Vernon looked defeated, but he was only playing possum. Judge Dwight prompted him.

"What sort of evidence, Mr. Wedge?"

"It's a demonstration, Your Honor," he said weakly. "In my opinion, it will clearly establish my client's guilt or innocence. But if the court rules—"

"Very well, Mr. Wedge, you may proceed."

Quickly, Vernon undid the clasps of the black box in front of him. He removed the wide-mouthed beaker, and then the foil lid that covered it. He brought the murky solution to the bench that held the trial exhibits.

"And what is this?" Judge Dwight said.

"This, Your Honor, is a chemical solution specifically formulated for the detection of blood."

The courtroom buzzed; on the prosecution's side of the room, there was a hurried consultation.

Vernon faced the jurors.

"Ladies and gentlemen, Exhibit A in this case is the knife which presumably killed Kenneth Tarcher. This is the knife which was in the possession of Benjamin Blesker the night of the slaying. Yet not one shred of testimony has been heard during this trial concerning the vital factor of *blood*."

He picked up the knife, and sprung the long, shining blade.

"This knife!" he said, waving it in the air. "Look at it carefully. It has never left the court's possession since my client's arrest. Yet this clean, shiny blade can still tell a story of guilt or innocence. For as every biochemist knows, there is an infallible test which can determine whether an object of such porous metal has *ever* been stained with even one drop of blood!"

He poised the knife over the mouth of the beaker.

"Ladies and gentlemen, I intend to prove once and for all whether I have been defending a boy falsely accused, or a lying murderer. I intend to dip this blade in the solution. If it turns pink—you must punish him for his guilt. If it remains clear—you must do what is just, and set him free."

Slowly, he brought the knife down.

"Your Honor!"

Wickers was on his feet, and Vernon halted.

"Your Honor, objection! Objection!"

"Yes, Mr. Wickers?"

Wickers' eyes flashed angrily. "Defense counsel is acting improperly. The police laboratory has already made the standard benzidine test of the weapon and found no bloodstains on the blade. We admit that the knife has been cleansed—"

"Your Honor," Vernon said loudly, "the sensitivity of this test far exceeds the benzidine—"

"This performance is irrelevant, immaterial, and completely improper!" Wickers whirled to the jury.

"At no time during this trial has the prosecution denied the absence of blood on Benjamin Blesker's knife. Any so-called "test" that corroborates this is completely gratuitous, and is intended as pure theatrics to mislead and befuddle the jury! I demand this farcical demonstration be stopped!"

There was a moment's silence. Vernon looked up at the judge hopefully, waiting.

Dwight folded his hands.

"Mr. Wedge, I'm afraid you're not in a position to qualify as an expert in forensic chemistry. And, as Mr. Wickers says, mere corroboration of the police laboratory report is gratuitous evidence that cannot be properly admitted. Therefore, the objection is sustained."

"But Your Honor—"

"Sustained," Judge Dwight said gravely. "You cannot make the test, Mr. Wedge."

His summation was the briefest of his career.

"I believe Benjamin Blesker is innocent," he said wearily. "I believe this because of a test I was not permitted to make. This boy knew that the results of this test might have condemned him, yet he told me to proceed. No guilty man would have allowed it; no innocent man would have had it any other way."

The jury was out less than an hour. When they returned, they declared that Benjamin Blesker was innocent.

Vernon was permitted the use of an adjoining chamber for a meeting with his client. It wasn't a victory celebration. The boy seemed stunned, and the happiness in old man Blesker's face looked more like sorrow. When the lawyer entered the room, he stood up shakily and held out his hand.

"God bless you," he whispered. "Bless you for what you did."

"I didn't come to be congratulated," Vernon said coldly. "I wanted to see you both for another reason."

The bailiff entered, and placed the beaker on the desk. When he left, Vernon took the knife out of his pocket, and put it down beside the beaker. The old man picked it up and looked at the weapon as if he had never seen it before.

"Wickers was right," Vernon said flatly. "What I did out there was theatrics. I didn't want to make the demonstration; I was counting on the prosecution halting it."

"You didn't want to?" Blesker said blankly. "You didn't want to make the test?"

"I could have gotten an expert, a real one, like Doc Hagerty. But I didn't want to take the chance; if this stuff had turned red . . ." He looked at the beaker and frowned. "No," he said. "The risk was too great. If Wickers had played along, I would have been forced to do it. But I figured they would object, and the jury would be impressed the right way. They were, thank God."

Blesker let out a long sigh.

"But now there's something we have to do," Vernon said. "Something to satisfy us all."

"What do you mean?"

Vernon looked at the boy. Benjy wouldn't meet his eyes.

"I still don't know the truth," the lawyer said. "I don't know it, and neither do you. Only Benjy here knows it."

"You can't mean that! You said yourself—"

"Never mind what I said out there. There's only one way we can really know, Mr. Blesker."

He held out his hand.

"Give me the knife, Mr. Blesker. We're going to make the test the judge wouldn't allow. For our own sakes."

"But why?" the old man cried. "What difference does it make?"

"*Because I want to know!* Even if you don't, Mr. Blesker, I want to know!"

"Give me the knife," Vernon said.

Blesker picked up the knife. He touched its cool blade thoughtfully.

"Of course," he said.

Then, slowly, he drew the blade deliberately across the back of his hand. The sharp edge bit deep. Blood welled like a crimson river in the cut and stained his hand, his cuff, his sleeve, the surface of the desk. He looked at the wound sadly, indifferently, and then handed the dripping weapon to the attorney.

"Make your test," he said dreamily. "Make your test now, Mr. Wedge."

And as Vernon stared at him, he removed a crumpled handkerchief from his pocket and wound it about his injured hand. Then he took his son's arm, and they left the room together.

THE ARTIFICIAL LIAR

William Brittain

Marley was dead, to begin with.

Major Orin Watkins, chief of security for the government's Biological Research Center No. 27, was familiar with most of Charles Dickens' works; however, he never expected to have Marley's demise reported to him in his official capacity. Dickens' *A Christmas Carol,* he believed, should be left to nineteenth century London. There was no place for the defunct partner of old Scrooge in The Center, a thoroughly modern complex of buildings occupying almost a hundred acres, where chemists and biologists with astronomical IQ's spent their working hours developing vaccines and antitoxins against diseases that in some cases hadn't been developed yet.

Life had been simpler for Scrooge; he had never heard of germ warfare, but it's unlikely that the old miser, had he put in an appearance, could have come within fifty feet of the gates. It would have been the job of Orin Watkins' men to keep him away from The Center. Those who did enter were constantly screened to within an inch of their lives. Orin himself was required to present the proper passes to the guard at the gate each day. No, Scrooge, Bob Cratchit, et al., were far better off nestled between the covers of a book.

Still, old Marley was as dead as a doornail.

Orin looked across the desk at the small man seated opposite. Augustine Lanier, his wrinkled old face reflecting anxiety and puzzlement, might have been himself a Dickens character. Not Scrooge, of course, not even Micawber. Augustine was too kindly for the one and too slender for the other. Barkis, that was it. Augustine was the very image of Barkis as Orin pictured the old wagoner after reading *David Copperfield*. Even though he was little more than a file clerk at The Center, Augustine was the most conscientious of workers. Like Barkis, Augustine, too, was willin'.

"Marley was my pet canary," explained Augustine softly. "It was probably my imagination, but it seemed to me when I bought him that he resembled a picture I'd seen of Marley's ghost. And now he's dead, sir."

Orin would never get used to having men twenty years his senior call him 'sir.' "Augustine, I'm sorry your pet died," he said. "But is that the only reason you came to see me? I watched you outside the office. You must have paced up and down for twenty minutes before you decided to come in. I thought you wanted to talk about something serious."

"It is serious, Mr. Watkins." Augustine Lanier slid still further down into his chair and peered dolefully at Orin over the tops of his steel-rimmed spectacles. "You see, I believe I should be relieved of my duties here at The Center. I might be something of a security risk in the program."

Orin looked at the older man in surprise. Augustine was one of the first employees taken on when The Center was constructed. He'd passed his security check with flying colors, according to the records. Past history, intelligence and psychological tests, polygraph results—all indicated a spotless reputation. Granted that The Center, dealing with the most deadly of pathogenic organisms, needed to be ultraselective in its choice of employees. Still, Augustine Lanier a security risk? Never.

"Look, Augustine, your pet died," said Orin finally, "but that's no reason to go into a blue funk and quit on us. Take the rest of the day off. Visit the pet stores in town. Buy another bird. You'll soon forget Marley."

"Oh, it's not just that Marley died that has me worried, sir." Augustine shook his head emphatically. "You see, he was strangled."

"Strangled? How in blazes did he manage to strangle himself?"

"Oh, Marley didn't do it himself, sir. It was no accident."

"You mean you—"

"I—I don't know." Augustine removed a handkerchief from his hip pocket and began pressing it into a ball between his palms. "That's part of the problem. And Marley's death was just the first incident. These last few days have been so strange. I think perhaps I'm losing touch with reality, Mr. Watkins."

Augustine made this last statement in an almost apologetic tone, as if somehow he were letting down not only Orin but the whole research center. One hand, containing the ball of handkerchief, rubbed at his eyes. "I'm sorry about disturbing you, sir," he continued, "but I thought you'd need to know."

That the old man had come in at all was a tribute to his faithfulness to The Center, Orin decided. How many people could admit the possibility of a mental breakdown, even to themselves? "Look, Augustine," he said gently, "suppose you begin at the beginning. Now, tell me what's been so strange about these last few days?" Surreptitiously he pressed a stud at the edge of his desk. A concealed microphone in the onyx pen set on the desk began ingesting Lanier's words and feeding them to the electronic tape moving between its reels in the bottom drawer.

"It began last Friday, sir." Augustine's voice reminded Orin of one of his own sons, telling how a window had been broken with a slingshot. "It was in the morning, and I was afraid I'd be late for work. Generally, Mrs. Carrigan—she owns the house in town where I rent my room—would wake me if I was in danger of oversleeping, but she's gone to visit relatives and won't be back until the end of the month. And Sergeant Pomeroy—he's the other roomer—he's off on a fishing trip until later this week. So you see, I was alone in the house, and I guess I just forgot to set the alarm."

Orin wondered if he would ever come to the point. "Pomeroy," he said conversationally, "that's Jerry Pomeroy, one of the guards at the west gate, isn't it?"

"Yes, sir," nodded Augustine. "At any rate, when I left the house and went to my car, I found I'd forgotten my keys. That happens rather often, sir. Sorry I'm so absent-minded."

"Just so nobody else gets hold of them," said Orin. "With your keys, anybody who managed to get inside could go almost anywhere, except the culture rooms, of course."

"Oh, Mr. Watkins!" Augustine looked shocked. "They've never been out of my possession for more than a few seconds. Honestly, sir."

"Okay, Augustine. Okay. Get on with your story."

"I went back into the house and up to my room. That's when I found him."

"Him? You mean Marley?"

"Yes, sir. Lying right in the middle of the carpet, he was. And he'd been strangled—with my keys."

Orin shook his head in confusion. "Strangled with keys," he said slowly. "I don't get that, Augustine."

"Oh, I'm sorry, sir. It wasn't with the keys exactly. I keep my key ring attached to a chain, and it was the chain that was wrapped around Marley's neck. It was so tight it almost beheaded the poor thing."

As he began to speak, Orin became the soul of sweet reasonableness. "It could happen," he said. "When you went out, the bird got loose. It fluttered around the room, and somehow it got tangled in your key chain."

"I suppose it could have happened that way, except—"

"Except what?"

"The chain hadn't just been wrapped around Marley's neck. It was knotted."

Orin sat back, expelling his breath loudly. "No chance that the bird could have—"

"None, Mr. Watkins. It was a square knot."

Odd, but nothing to do with the security of The Center, of course. That is, unless Augustine was going dotty and had at some time blacked out and strangled the bird himself.

"You mentioned a while back that the death of the bird was just the 'first incident,'" said Orin suddenly.

"What did you mean by that, Augustine?"

"Well, the next thing was the tools in my medicine cabinet, files, to be exact."

"Files?"

"Yes. You see, I had a headache all day Friday, thinking about Marley and wondering how it could have happened. So when I got home that afternoon, I decided to take a couple of aspirin. Mrs. Carrigan lets me keep a bottle in the medicine cabinet in the bathroom. I'm often subject to headaches."

"Go on."

"Well, I went to the second floor bathroom and drew a glass of water. Then I opened the medicine cabinet. Oh, the crashing and banging was terrible."

"What crashing and banging?"

"When the files fell out. Long round ones they were, of blued steel. I believe they're the type called 'rattail.'"

"Well?" Orin nodded expectantly.

"That's about all. But isn't a medicine cabinet an odd place to keep files? Especially so many. There must have been at least two dozen. I'm afraid a couple of them chipped the sink rather badly. Mrs. Carrigan will be quite upset when she returns and finds the damage."

"And how did these files get into the medicine cabinet?" asked Orin, a touch of sarcasm filtering into his voice.

"I—I don't know, sir. They certainly weren't there the previous evening, and yet I was the only person in the house. That's what worries me, Mr. Watkins. Is it possible that, without realizing it, I put them there myself?"

"Umm. Possible, I suppose. It's strange, though, that you'd have no recollection at all."

"It almost sounds as if I might be . . . well . . . going out of my mind. Doesn't it?"

"That'd be up to the medics to decide, Augustine," said Orin. "But I wouldn't worry about it. There has to be some logical explanation. Besides, I'd expect a man on the verge of insanity to experience hallucinations;

visions, loss of reality, that sort of thing."

Augustine took a deep breath and let it out with a shudder.

Orin, seeing the old man's reactions, cocked an eyebrow. "Have you experienced any hallucinations, Augustine?"

"I—I really don't know."

"What do you mean, you don't know? Explain yourself." Orin's voice was sharper than he intended it to be.

"It was Saturday evening, Mr. Watkins. I went out for a walk, nowhere in particular. I was having trouble sleeping, what with Marley, and then the files tumbling out of the medicine cabinet. I'd left the house about eleven-thirty, so it must have been after midnight when it happened."

"When what happened?"

"I had stopped under a street lamp to light my pipe. As I struck the match, I suddenly realized there was a man standing beside me. I hadn't heard him approach. He must have been wearing rubber-soled shoes."

"Did the man try to attack you? Did he demand money or anything like that?"

"Oh, no! In fact, he tipped his hat in the most polite manner. It's just that when he removed the hat, and the light hit his face, I saw that he was wearing a mask."

"A mask?"

"Yes, sir. It was one of those rubber things that fit over the entire head. Fairly scared the life out of me, it did. You see, the mask was of a . . . a werewolf. Not only that, but the man suddenly went down on his hands and knees and began howling at the moon. Then, just as quickly, he got to his feet, replaced his hat, shook my hand and vanished into the darkness."

Orin chuckled. "That one's easily explained, at least," he said with a smile. "Either someone coming home from a costume party or a practical joker. Drunk, probably."

"Perhaps. But after the first two incidents, meeting that man didn't do my nerves any good, I can tell you that. And I've been unable to locate anybody else in the area who either saw the man or even heard of such a thing happening."

"It is kind of screwy, but not impossible. Is there anything else, Augustine?"

"Yes, Mr. Watkins. One thing more. It happened just last night—or perhaps this morning. It's hard to say."

Orin could see that Augustine was visibly shaken by the events that had happened. His thin arms twitched alarmingly, and he seemed on the verge of tears.

"Yesterday evening, I cleaned my room, sir; vacuuming, dusting, the whole thing. At the time I went to bed, everything was in its proper place. You've got to believe that, Mr. Watkins. You've got to!"

"Okay, Augustine, okay. Nobody's doubting your word. Go on with your story."

"Yes, of course. I'm sorry to lose control of myself. At any rate, I locked the door and went to bed. But this morning when I got up, I found . . . I found . . ." Augustine suddenly covered his face with the handkerchief and burst into horrible and uncontrolled sobbing.

For several minutes, the silence of Orin's office was broken only by the pitiful moans of the old man. Finally, with a tremendous effort of will, he became quiet. Bending over, he picked up a roll of paper from the floor beside the chair and tossed it onto Orin's desk.

"That, Mr. Watkins. I found that on the floor of my room. Held flat with books from my shelves, it was. But I didn't put it there. I've never even seen it before this morning. I swear it, sir! I don't know where it came from!"

Orin unrolled the stiff paper. It was a poster of some kind. The picture was of a military man in his late fifties or early sixties, wearing the uniform of a World War I soldier. The handsomeness of the rugged face with its neat moustache and coolly competent expression was set off by the brilliant display of campaign ribbons and the general's four stars on his uniform. Orin read the few words below the picture: GENERAL JOHN J. "BLACK JACK" PERSHING, commander in chief of the American Expeditionary Force in Europe.

"Nothing frightening about the picture, at least," said Orin finally.

"That's not the point, Mr. Watkins. I never owned such a picture. How did it get into my room? First, my canary was killed. After that, the files in the medicine cabinet and the man with that hideous mask. And now this. At first, I—I thought about not saying anything to anybody, but—"

"Yeah, that's what ninety-nine people out of a hundred would do. But you did the right thing, Augustine. Only . . . Oh, dammit!" Orin balled up a sheet of paper from his desk and hurled it into a corner of the small office.

"Are you all right, Mr. Watkins?"

"Yeah, Augustine. It's just that you're too nice a guy for what I've got to do to you."

"What do you mean, sir?"

"Look, you've told me some pretty wild things. They just don't make any sense. For what it's worth, I don't think you're going screwball. On the other hand, I'm not a doctor. I'm a security officer, and regardless of my personal feelings, my first duty's to the safety and security of The Center. Right?"

"I suppose so, but—"

"Don't interrupt me while I'm griping. Now, if these things had happened to one of the scientists here, I might think somebody was trying to drive him insane. But frankly, Augustine, your job as a clerk just doesn't have that high a priority. Let's face it, if you disappeared tomorrow, you could be replaced without too much trouble. Furthermore, you don't know enough about the operations here for you to give anybody really vital material, I don't mean to hurt your feelings, but that's the way things are."

"I'm aware of that, Mr. Watkins."

"All right, then, if we eliminate the idea that some unknown party's trying to get you out of The Center, what's left?"

Augustine stared bleakly at the floor. "What you're trying to say is that I either imagined these things or I did them myself. Isn't that it?"

"Yeah, but . . .Oh, hell!" Orin picked up the telephone on his desk and poised an index finger over the dial. "I'm going to have to keep you here at The Center, Augustine," he said. "You'll be under guard, and the doctors will be dropping in fairly often. I'll make you as comfortable as I can, but no word will be allowed out as to your whereabouts. And if you're thinking about exercising your constitutional rights to habeas corpus, forget it. This is a top-secret government project, not a courtroom."

"Please don't worry yourself about my welfare," said Augustine. "I understood the consequences when I walked in here."

Orin opened his mouth to speak and then abruptly closed it. What more was there to say? He spun the telephone dial around angrily.

After turning Augustine Lanier over to two guards who were given strict orders not to let the old man out of their sight until he was given clearance, Orin went to the cafeteria and ate a lunch that could have been boiled cardboard for all the enjoyment he got from it. Returning to his office, he flopped into his swivel chair, spun it away from the desk and considered a ground plan of The Center that was mounted on the wall.

There was the sound of drumming feet outside the building, and he turned to watch through the window as the perimeter guards changed. After a formal exchange of salutes, the new men took their places at the small booths by the gates, while those who had been on duty the previous four hours returned to the barracks just below the office. There, the men who lived on the base could read, talk or catch up on their sleep while the noncommissioned officers who had rooms in town dashed out through the gates to catch a bus. Until eight o'clock that evening, their time was their own.

Orin frowned suddenly, glancing from the window back to the floor plan. There was something he hadn't noticed before. Easy enough to remedy, of course, but a possible breach of security, just the same.

There was a knock on the door. "Come in," Orin shouted impatiently.

The man who waddled through the door had his military shirt fully unbuttoned and was scratching at his hairy chest with one massive hand. Between his teeth was clenched a pipe with a bowl roughly the size of a coffee cup. If Colonel Timothy Doherty, The Center's chief medical officer, hadn't been such a superb physician, he'd have long since been drummed out of the service simply for being a slob. Orin, however, liked Doherty immensely. The fat doctor added a dash of Irish *joie de vivre* to The Center's severely formal military routines.

"Thought you'd like to hear how I'm getting on with your Mr. Lanier," said Doherty, settling into a chair and at the same time dribbling burning embers from his pipe onto the carpet.

"Yeah, Tim. In a minute."

"What do you mean, in a minute? I thought you asked me to let you know as soon as I'd finished looking at him."

"Just take a look at this chart first, will you?" Orin jabbed a finger toward the ground plan. "We're right here, and the guards who just came off duty are downstairs."

"A fair assessment," nodded Doherty, "especially as they're making enough racket down there to wake the dead."

"But Tim, they're still inside The Center."

Doherty spread his hands wide. "A marvelous bit of deduction, Orin," he said. "What do you do for an encore? Locate Judge Crater?"

"C'mon, be serious," replied Orin. "I want to see if I've got this figured right. Now, we allow the guards who live in town to go out of The Center when they come off duty, without checking them any too closely. If one of them wanted to take something from The Center, he wouldn't have much trouble smuggling it out."

"Take something? And what would one of your own men be wanting to take?"

"There are people who'd be willing to pay quite a bit for information about The Center's activities."

"You mean you don't even trust the guards?"

"In this job, I don't trust anybody. It would be a big temptation. Look, the record-storage area is in the other end of this building. What would prevent one of the guards from walking out of the barracks and into the record area when he came off duty, instead of going right out through the gate?"

"Well, for one thing, somebody'd see him. It's broad daylight. And for the second thing, the record department's always kept firmly locked."

"But if it were night? And the guard had a key?"

"Oh, I suppose he could get inside under those circumstances. If he wanted to, that is."

"Then he could look into the filing cabinets at every experiment we've ever done here. Even photograph them, if he had a camera."

"Now, wait a minute, Orin. There's a special watchman right outside the room where the records themselves are kept, and even he doesn't have a key to the rooms or the filing cabinets."

"Okay, but let's say our man comes along this passage. He'd be out of sight of the watchman until the last minute. He could hit the watchman with something and—"

"And even assuming he got all those locks open, the moment the watchman woke up and identified him, he'd be hunted by every policeman in the country. And treason's still a capital offense, I believe."

"What if he wore a mask?"

"What if! What if!" Doherty relit his pipe and peered through the smoke at Orin. "If the thing is really bothering you, just keep the perimeter guards under observation until they actually leave The Center."

"Yeah, I think I'll suggest that to the commanding officer." Orin spun about and faced the plump doctor. "Now, what about Lanier?"

"I've no official diagnosis yet, but just between us tin soldiers, he's as sane as you or me. Except after hearing you talk, I'm not so sure about you." With a sly grin, Doherty peered from under bushy brows at Orin. "By the way, Lanier's canary really is dead, you know," he said offhandedly.

"Oh? How did you find that out?"

"Lanier mentioned he'd buried it in the back yard. I sent a couple of men out to his rooming house, and they dug up the corpse. Its neck had been broken."

"Sounds like you're doing my job for me," said Orin, grinning.

"All in the line of duty. We've got the bird's body and the picture of Pershing. At least we know those two things aren't imaginary. I strongly suspect, Orin-me-boy, that I'll be forced to give that man a clean bill of health."

"He'll still have to be let go unless we can explain those incidents logically."

"Have you thought of trying the polygraph?"

"The lie detector? What good would that do? If Augustine's lying, he's an automatic security risk. And if not, the things that happened are so suspicious that he'd still be thrown out. What's the difference?" Orin asked diffidently.

"We might get some insight as to what's on his mind. Orin, you learned to operate the polygraph during security training. You know it isn't perfect. That's why it's not acceptable as evidence."

"Except here at The Center," answered Orin. "If anybody's polygraph chart doesn't stay within reasonable limits, he's out. It may not be fair, but security is maintained."

"All right, but we both know the lie detector can't peer into anybody's brain to see if he's lying. All the machine does is measure bodily responses. A pressure cuff measures blood pressure and pulse. A tube around the chest gets the dope on respiration depth and frequency, and electrodes on the fingers tell how much the subject is perspiring. All these are automatically graphed on a chart."

"Right out of the textbook, Tim. Then the subject is given neutral questions or words—'cat' or 'dog' or something like that to test his usual reactions. Only when Augustine heard the word 'canary', his graph would go right off the paper because of what happened to—Holy Saint Jude Thaddeus!"

"Orin, you're as white as a sheet. Are you all right? Do you want me to get you something?"

"Just the phone." Orin grabbed at the instrument, index finger stabbing at the dial. "Sergeant Jennings, I want Mr. Lanier brought to my office right away," he barked into the mouthpiece. "On the double!" He slammed the receiver back into its cradle.

"I take it you're onto something," said Doherty calmly. "Or are you just trying for a coronary right here in your office?"

"Oh," muttered Orin, his lips pulled back tight against his teeth. "That clever son-of-a . . . This is one for the books, all right, and it might have worked if Augustine had just kept quiet like any ordinary person. But instead, he came to me. Bless his conscientious heart, he came to me!"

"I think I'll stay," said Doherty. "I've nothing but two cases of blistered feet this morning, anyway. And you'd better be making some sense out of this mishmash, or I've got another room waiting for you, right next to Lanier's."

Three minutes later, Augustine Lanier slowly shuffled into Orin's office and nodded nervously to the two men. Orin offered him a chair.

"Augustine," Orin said when the old man was seated, "I think I've got some good news for you. I think I know the meaning of the things that happened to you."

"All of them, sir?" asked Augustine softly.

"Every blasted one. Listen. A few moments ago, I described to Colonel Doherty here, how one of the perimeter guards might possibly enter the records area and take material out."

"Really, Mr. Watkins? That's where I work—or where I used to work. I thought it was quite closely guarded."

"No, not only would it be possible for someone to get in, but I think somebody's actually planning to do it. And there are places in the world where the information in those records would be worth a bundle."

"Oh, I hope you'll be able to catch him, sir. Many of the envelopes I've put in the cabinets have been labeled Top Secret."

"I don't think we'll have any trouble on that score.

You see, I think the thief plans on staying on right here at The Center. He's going to try and make it seem as if someone else is the guilty person. You, Augustine."

"Me? I don't understand. How?"

"Over to you, Tim." Orin turned his chair to face Doherty. "If a theft like the one I've described actually took place, what would be the first thing I'd do?"

"Oh, seal off the area. Ascertain what was actually broken into. Make up excuses to the commanding officer for your blunders."

"Yes, but when I started questioning suspects, what then? I'd use the polygraph, Tim. The lie detector. And I'd start with the people who had access to the room. Augustine, here, would be one of the first people tested."

"I still don't get it," said Doherty.

"Think, Tim." Orin turned to the old man. "Augustine, you were set up for a theft of records that may take place tonight, or certainly within the next couple of days. You were going to be the patsy for this job. You'd have been turned into perhaps the world's first artificial liar."

"It's all very confusing, sir."

"Tim," Orin gestured toward the doctor, "imagine Augustine strapped into the lie detector. The machine is attached to his body. His blood pressure, pulse, respiration and skin conductivity are all being monitored. I begin by asking his name or how he feels. Anything to put him at ease so we can get a proper reading.

"But now, we agree that the real thief would have access to keys to the record area. So, after a few innocent words, I say 'keys.' "

In his chair, Augustine Lanier jerked involuntarily. The color drained from his face. "Oh, poor Marley," he whispered. "And with my own key chain."

"Saint Patrick, protect us!" murmured Doherty. "With a reaction like that, he'd send the lie detector needles right through the wall." He scratched his head doubtfully. "But what about the other things, Orin? The files in the medicine cabinet, for instance?"

"Try the words 'file cabinet,' Tim."

"And the werewolf getup would provide a reaction to 'mask.' But what about General Pershing?"

" 'Black Jack.' The watchman would have to be slugged with something, remember? We'd be given a perfect suspect. Not because Augustine had done anything wrong, but because he'd been psychologically conditioned to respond to the very words we were bound to use in our investigation. Meanwhile, as we concentrated on Augustine, the guilty party would be laughing up his sleeve at us. However, in one way, Augustine didn't act the way he was expected to. Instead of keeping those odd events to himself, he told me about them."

"And the real thief, the one who's been doing all these things to Mr. Lanier? Have you got him pegged, too?" asked Doherty.

Orin leaned back, grinning. "Sure," he said. "Augustine, you've been telling me all along that for the past few days you'd been alone in the rooming house. You weren't, you know."

"You mean my landlady—"

Orin shook his head. "She'd hardly qualify as a guard here," he said. "But—"

"Sergeant Pomeroy," breathed Augustine, his eyes wide with amazement. "His room's right across the hall from mine."

"Now you're catching on, Augustine. You see, I don't believe Pomeroy ever went on his fishing trip. He may have left the house while you watched, but it's my guess he stashed his luggage somewhere and sneaked back. He's been lying concealed in his room ever since. You said you'd forgotten your keys several times. He could have slipped over to your room and made clay casts of them in seconds, before you returned to pick them up. Since you're a file clerk, those keys would have let him into any part of the record area. The same thing with Marley; how long does it take to kill a tiny bird? He just waited until you'd forgotten your keys once more, came into your room, opened the cage, and that was that. The other occurrences would have been even easier to set up. All Pomeroy had to do was wait until you were out of the house and he could set up your room any way he liked."

"An interesting theory, Orin-me-boy," said Doherty. "Going to be a bit difficult to prove, though, isn't it?"

"No trouble at all," said Orin.

Two nights later, a figure dressed in a dark shirt and pants unlocked the side door of The Center's record area, opened the door, and quickly slipped inside. He pushed the door shut behind him. As he turned, someone in the darkness whipped away the black bandanna handkerchief which had been wrapped around his face. Startled, he dropped a large ring of keys to the floor just as somebody turned on the overhead lights. In front of the man, four soldiers held their bayoneted rifles at the ready.

"Welcome, Sergeant Pomeroy," said Orin Watkins, placing the black handkerchief carefully in his pocket. "We've been waiting for you."

FOR MONEY RECEIVED

(Novelette)

Fletcher Flora

The rain came straight down into the alley, and I sat with my back to my desk and watched the rain. It was not an afternoon for being out and doing something. Besides, I had nowhere to go and nothing to do. If I had somewhere to go more often, and something to do when I got there, I would be able to watch the rain come down past a front window instead of a back, into a street instead of an alley. Provided, of course, that I went where I went and did what I did for clients who paid me a great deal more than my clients usually paid.

My name is Percy Hand, and I'm a private detective. My privacy is rarely invaded. This makes the rent a problem, but it gives me plenty of time to watch the rain come down into the alley on rainy days.

Someone was coming down the hall. My ears are big and my hearing is acute, so I tried to establish certain facts, just for fun, about the person approaching. It was apparent from the sharp, quick rhythm of the steps that the person was a woman, probably young. I decided from a more esoteric suggestion in the sound that this woman, whoever she was exactly, was a woman of pride and even arrogance. In her purse, moreover, was a checkbook in which she could write, if she chose, a withdrawal of six figures. To the left, I mean, of the decimal point. These last two deductions were wholly unwarranted by the evidence, and probably explain why I am not the best detective in the world, although not the worst. They assumed, that is, that poor women cannot be proud, which is palpably untrue. Anyhow, if she was rich, chances were a hundred to one that she was not coming to see me.

But I was wrong. My reception room door from the

hall opened and closed, releasing between the opening and the closing a brief, angry exclamation from a buzzer. The buzzer is cheaper than a receptionist, even though it is not as amusing, especially on rainy days. I got around my desk and out there in a hurry, before this client had time to walk out.

She was wearing a belted raincoat and holding in one hand a matching hat. Her hair was black and short and curling in the damp. She could look over a short man's head and a tall man's shoulder, excluding basketball players. At the end of nice legs was a pair of sensible brown shoes with flat heels. Inasmuch as I had heard her clearly in the hall, the shoes had to have leather heels.

"Are you Mr. Percy Hand?" she asked.

Her voice was modulated and musical, now with a quality of calculated coolness that could instantly change, I suspected, to calculated warmth or coldness as the occasion required.

After admitting that I was Percy Hand, I asked, "What can I do for you?" I scrutinized her curiously.

"I'm not certain." She looked around the shabby little room with obvious reservations. "I expected something different. Do all private detectives have offices like this?"

"Some do, some don't. It depends on how much money they make."

"I don't know that I like that. It must mean that you don't have many clients, and there is surely a reason. Why aren't you more successful?" She pointedly questioned.

"Happiness comes before success, I always say."

"It's a nice philosophy if you can afford it. On the other hand, you may be unsuccessful because you're honest. I have a notion that private detectives, in general, are not very reliable. Can you tell me if that is so?"

"Professional ethics prevents my answering."

"I heard that about you. That you're honest. Someone told me."

"My thanks to someone. Who, precisely?"

"I don't think I'll tell you. It doesn't matter. A

woman I know for whom you did something. She said that you were perfectly reliable, although not brilliant."

"My thanks is now qualified. I maintain that, properly motivated, I can be brilliant for short periods."

"Well, I'm not especially concerned about that. What I need is someone, on whose discretion I can rely, to do a simple job."

"I'm your man. Simple, discreet jobs are those at which I'm best."

"In that case, I'd better stay and tell you about it."

She began to unbuckle her belt, and I stepped forward, like a discreet and reliable gentleman, to help her off with her raincoat. Then I gestured toward the door to my office, and she went through the door ahead of me and helped herself to the chair at the end of the desk. She was wearing a simple brown wool dress that verified my intuitive conclusion that she was, if not actually rich, at least substantially endowed. She crossèd her legs and showed her knees, and I saw, just before sinking into my own chair behind the desk, that the knees were good.

"And now," I asked, "what is it that you want me to do, discreetly and simply?"

"First, I'd better tell you who I am. I haven't told you, have I?"

"You haven't."

"I'm Mrs. Benedict Coon. The third. My Christian name is Dulce, if it matters."

"It doesn't. Not yet. Chances are, it never will."

"My husband and I live at 15 Corning Place. Do you know who the Coons are?"

"Canned food for dogs and cats?"

"They're the ones. Isn't it absurd?"

"Oh, I don't know. I'm very hesitant about criticizing anything so profitable."

"Well, never mind. It's true that too much money, from whatever source, can cause one to do foolish things and get one into a great deal of trouble. That's why I'm here. My husband has been seeing another woman, and I want you to find out who she is and where she lives."

"Excuse me." I was already parting sadly from a fee

that might have been fat. "I don't do divorce work. I can refer you to another operator, if you like."

She laughed softly. "Such admirable scruples! No wonder you're so poor. But you misunderstand me. I have no wish for a divorce. I'm far too fond of being Mrs. Benedict Coon III. Do you think for a moment that I would voluntarily give up my position because of a ridiculous peccadillo on the part of my husband?"

I relaxed and recovered hope. The fat fee again became feasible.

"All right. Tell me exactly what you want me to do."

"I'm trying to, if you will only quit being difficult about things. Benedict is being blackmailed by the woman he has been seeing. I don't know why exactly, but I want you to find a way to stop it. That will be your job."

"What's this woman's name?"

"I heard him call her Myrna. That's all I know."

"You heard him? You mean you've seen him with her?"

"No, no. Nothing of the sort. I heard him talking with her on the telephone. I just happened to come home unexpectedly and pick up the downstairs extension while they were talking. That's how I know about the meeting tomorrow."

"What meeting? When? Where?"

"You know, I'm beginning to think you may be more capable than you seemed at first. From the way you go directly after the pertinent facts, I mean. Well, anyhow, they arranged to meet at three o'clock tomorrow in the Normandy Lounge. That's in the Hotel Stafford."

"I know where it is. What's the purpose of the meeting?" I asked.

"I'm coming to that as fast as I can. She has something that he wants to get back. Neither he nor she said what. Whatever it is, however, it's the reason he's been paying her money. Quite a lot of money, I gather. Now he wants to pay her a much larger amount for its final return, to end things once and for all. She agreed to meet him and talk about it."

"At the Normandy Lounge?"

"They'll meet there. Probably they'll go on to somewhere else."

"At three o'clock tomorrow afternoon?"

"Yes."

"Why not let him pay the amount, however much, and get the blackmail gimmick back, whatever it is? He can afford it."

"Of course he can. If it works out that way, I'm prepared to forget the whole thing. But how can I be sure that it will? If it falls through, if she's up to more tricks, I want to know who she is and where she lives, and how I can get Benedict free of her."

"Have you discussed this with your husband?"

"Oh, no! Certainly not! That would never do. He'd go all to pieces and spoil the chances of doing anything whatever. He's weak, you see, besides being a hopeless liar."

"You want me to be at the lounge and follow them if they leave?"

"Or follow her if she leaves without him. Will you do it?"

"Why not? Divorce is one thing, blackmail another."

"It's settled, then." She dug into her purse again and came out with a thin packet of lovely treasury notes which she laid on my desk, and which I picked up at once just to get the feel of them. "There's five hundred dollars there, a fair fee for an afternoon's work. If there's more work later, there will be more money. We'll discuss it if there is."

"How will I recognize your husband?"

"He's medium height, has blond hair. Not particularly distinctive, so you'd better know exactly what he'll be wearing. I'll be watching when he leaves the house, and I'll call immediately and give you a description. Will you be in your office?"

"I'll make a point of it."

She stood up and headed for the door. I followed her into the reception room and helped her on with her raincoat. When the hall door had closed behind her, I stood and listened with my big, acute ears to the sound of her receding footsteps. Then I returned to my office and stood at the window and looked through the rain, still falling, at the brick wall across the alley from me.

What order of events, I thought, had sent Dulce Coon here? What strange chance had put into my hands more money than they had held at once for a long, long time?

There were two approaches to the Normandy Lounge; one was directly from the street, an inducement to susceptible pedestrians, and the other was through the lobby of the Hotel Stafford and down a shallow flight of stairs. I entered from the street, filled with bright light after a gray day, and stopped just inside, while the door swung shut behind me with a soft pneumatic whisper. I waited until my pupils had dilated in adjustment to thick, scented darkness that was pricked here and there by points of light, and then I navigated slowly between tiny tables to an upholstered seat against the wall. Above the bar and behind the bartender was the illuminated dial of an electric clock. I ordered a glass of beer from a waitress who came to see what I wanted.

The clock said ten minutes till three. A canary was singing softly in a juke box, and the canary was so in love. Two men and a woman were lined up on stools at the bar. The woman was between the men, but she only talked with the one on her right, and the one on her left just sat and stared at his shadow in the mirror. Half a dozen men and women were scattered one to one at tables, holding hands and rubbing knees, and the murmur of their voices made a kind of choral accompaniment to the love-sick canary. Trade was slow, but the time was wrong. In a couple of hours, with the closing of offices and shops, things would pick up. The waitress delivered my glass of beer, and I began to nurse it.

He was wearing, Dulce Coon had said, a brown plaid jacket and brown slacks. His shirt was white, button-down collar, and his tie was fashionably narrow. He was medium height and his hair was blond, and so was the mustache that I might miss unless my eyes were as good as my ears. I couldn't miss him, she said, but I begged to differ. Jacket and slacks and all the rest were not distinctive and might apply to someone else. Not likely, she said, to someone else who would appear at three or shortly before. Not at all likely, she added, to someone else who would be joined in the lounge by a woman. I conceded, and here I was, Percy Hand on the alert, and there he was, sure enough, coming down the steps from the lobby at exactly two minutes till three by the clock.

He crawled onto a stool near the lobby entrance and ordered something in water, probably scotch or bourbon. I could see only his back, with a glancing shot at his profile now and then as his head turned. I tried to focus on the mirror for a better look, but there were bottles and glasses in the way, and faces there, besides, were only shadows. He was the one, though. No question about it. It was evident in his subtle suggestion of tense expectancy, his too-frequent references to the clock as the two minutes till three went to ten minutes past. His right hand held his glass. His left hand kept moving out to a bowl of salted peanuts on the bar. He was Benedict Coon III, and he was waiting for a woman named Myrna who was also, by informal indictment, a blackmailer. It was another drink and a quarter of a pound of peanuts later before she came. But then there she was, all at once, beside him.

She was onto the next stool before I was aware of her. Once aware, however, I was aware in spades, and if Benedict had been indiscreet with Myrna, I was not the one to blame him. You didn't even have to see her face to know that inciting indiscretions was, with her, a natural effect of observable causes. A little taller than average, she possessed, without going into censorable details, a full inventory of quality stock. Her hair, just short of her shoulders, was pale blond, almost white, and I would have sworn that it was natural, although it is impossible to tell, actually, in these days of superior artifice. She was wearing a dark red suit with a tight and narrow skirt, and the skirt rode well above her knees on nylon as she perched on the stool and crossed her legs. Suffice it to say that even the vital juices of Percy Hand came instantly to a simmer.

I preferred the scenery from where I was, but I had a job to do with priority over pleasure, and I had a bank account of five hundred dollars, minus pocket money, to remind me of it. So, ethical if nothing else, I moved with my glass to the bar. Leaving a pair of stools between me and them, I ordered another beer and cocked an acute ear, but I might as well have been wearing plugs. They said little to each other, and what they said, was said too softly to be understood. Naturally, I thought. They were scarcely on terms of innocent and amiable conversation, and nothing that was to pass between them could be passed openly in a public cocktail lounge. I wanted to turn my head and look at them directly, but I didn't think I'd better. I tried from closer range to see her clearly in the mirror, but I could only see enough of her face to know that the rest of her had no cause to be ashamed of it.

She was holding in her left hand, I saw sidewise, a pair of dark glasses that she had removed in the shadowy lounge—the Hollywood touch. She had ordered a martini, and she drank the martini slowly and ate the olive afterward. He said something to her, and she said something to him, and suddenly, in unison, they slipped off their stools and went up the shallow flight of stairs into the lobby. When I got there after them, they were headed directly for the doors on the far side. Her high, thin heels tapped out a brisk cadence as they crossed a border of terrazzo beyond a thick rug.

Outside, they crossed the street at an angle in the middle of the block, and I assumed that they were going to a garage, convenient to the hotel, where he must have left his car. My own, such as it was, was down the block in the opposite direction, occupying a slot at the curb that I had found by luck. I went down to it, got in and started the engine, and waited. They would have to come past me, I knew, because it was a one-way street. In a few minutes they came, in a gray sedan. I swung in behind it and tagged along.

They were in no hurry, scrupulously minding the posted limits. They never got separated from me by more than an intruding car or two, and I was able to make all the lights that they made, although I had to run a couple on the yellow. We passed through the congested downtown area, turning east after a while onto an east-west boulevard.

Their car picked up speed, moving briskly down a gauntlet of fancy apartment buildings. I had a notion that one of them might be the sedan's destination, but I was wrong in my notion, which is not rare. It ran the gauntlet without stopping or turning, and it came pretty soon to an oblique intersection with a northeast-southwest thoroughfare. A red light held it there in the left-turn lane, and I waited behind it in the same lane. Between us were two cars that had slipped into the traffic along the way.

I kept watching the light, which was a long one, and I thought it would never change. At last it did, and the traffic in the other lanes began to move. Not ours. The sedan sat, and we all sat behind it. Drivers in cars ahead and behind began to lean on their horns in a demonstration of annoyance, but the gray car ignored the demonstrators with impervious arrogance. It simply waited and waited until it was ready to move, and it wasn't ready until the instant the light went yellow. Then it shot into the intersection, wheeled left with whining tires, and was gone down the thoroughfare before I could curse or cry or even cluck.

Other drivers, no doubt, wondered what had promoted this deliberate outrage. Not I. I knew that old Percy had been neatly slipped, and I wondered why. I wondered, that is, why the pair in the gray sedan should even have been aware of my presence on earth, let alone on their collective tail. Was I guilty of glaring error? Had, perhaps, my ears flapped at the bar when I strained to hear their conversation, what little there had been? Did even ethical private detectives have a distinctive smell of which they were unaware? And, grim reflection, was I now entitled to keep all of the five C's that I had been paid to do a simple job that I had simply failed to do? It was true that no conditions had been attached to the fee, but it was equally true that I hadn't earned it, or even enough of it to buy a hamburger sandwich. In fact, I conceded bitterly, I ought to pay damages.

Well, no good in crying. No good, either, in trying to run down the other car. I had been slipped, and that was that. The only thing to do was to find a phone and call Dulce Coon and make a full and abject confession of professional idiocy. I crossed the intersection, found a turn, and made my way downtown again by another route. The only telephone I could think of that wouldn't cost me a dime was the one in my office. I went there and sat at my desk backwards and looked at the brick wall across the alley. I thought about what had happened, and how I could explain it in a way that would salvage at least some of my dignity, if none of my fee.

Something had gone wrong, that was clear, and it didn't take a better brain than mine to know what. I had been expected and spotted and duped, that was what. But how? And why? And just when? The best explanation, so far as I could see, was that Dulce Coon, sometime between yesterday and today, had somehow given the business away. For that matter, it was possible that she had been followed through the rain to my office. If so, she was partly responsible for my fiasco, and didn't that give me a legitimate claim to my fee? Well, there was a way to find out. The way was at hand, and there was no point in waiting any longer to take it. Turning around to my desk in my swivel, I consulted the directory and dialed a number, and somewhere in the house at 15 Corning Place a telephone was answered by someone that I assumed to be a maid.

Was Mrs. Coon at home?

Sorry. Mrs. Coon wasn't. Who was calling, please?

Mr. Percy Hand was calling. When was Mrs. Coon expected?

That wasn't known. Would Mr. Hand care to leave a message?

Mr. Hand wouldn't.

I tried again an hour later, after five o'clock. Still no luck. The same maid gave me the same answers. This time, I asked her to have Mrs. Coon call Mr. Hand immediately upon her return home. The maid agreed, but the tone of her voice implied a polite skepticism of Mrs. Coon's compliance.

I went downstairs to a lunchroom and bought a couple of corned beef sandwiches and a pint of coffee in a cardboard container. I carried the sandwiches and the coffee back to my office and had my dinner, pardon the expression, at my desk. I had what was left of the coffee with a couple of cigarettes. The container was drained and the second butt stubbed when the telephone began to ring, and it was Dulce Coon at last.

"I had word to call you," she said. "What do you want?"

"I tried twice before to get you, but you weren't home. I thought you'd want a report."

"Go ahead and report. Did you see Benedict and the woman?"

"I saw them. They met at the bar in the Normandy Lounge, just as you said they would."

"Did they leave together?"

"They did, two highballs and a martini later. They walked from the hotel to a garage and drove off in a gray sedan."

"That's Benedict's car. Did you follow them?"

"After a fashion."

"What do you mean by that? Either you did or you didn't. Where did they go?"

"Briefly, I lost them. Or, to put it more accurately, they lost me. They ran a yellow and left a long line of traffic, including me, sitting on a red."

"Why should they do that?"

"A good question. I was about to ask it myself. That tricky business at the light was planned. They did it to shake a tail, and I'd like to know how they knew they had one. Did you give it away?"

"Certainly not."

"Somehow or other, he must have got onto it. Are you sure you weren't followed to my office yesterday?"

"There was no reason why I should have been."

"You said you overheard his conversation with the woman on an extension. Maybe he knew you were listening."

"That's absurd. If he had heard me lift the receiver,

he'd have quit talking, and I didn't hang up until after he did."

"Nevertheless, he knew. Somehow he knew he was being tailed."

"Obviously. Aren't you, perhaps, just trying to make an excuse for yourself? You must have bungled the job by making yourself conspicuous or something. I thought following people was a kind of basic thing that detectives learned from their primer. It seems to me that any good one ought to know how to do it."

"All right. So I'll have to go back to kindergarten. Don't worry, though. I'll see that most of the fee is returned to you."

"That won't be necessary. I offered the fee without conditions."

"It's a lot of money for practically nothing."

"I've spent more for less. I can afford it. Besides, this may not be the end of it. If there's something very simple that you can do for me later, I'll get in touch."

"In the meanwhile," I said, "I'll be studying my primer."

She hung up, and I hung up, and we left it at that. I tried to think of something simple to do with the evening, and the simplest thing I could think of was to go home and sleep, something which is even pre-primer in its simplicity. So I bought a pint of bourbon and took it to bed with me. Sometime after ten I went to sleep, and slept until almost seven the next morning.

At my office, I read a morning paper. Then I had a client who had a minor job to offer, and the job, which doesn't matter, took me away for the rest of the morning. After a businessman's special, I returned to the office and found the reception room full of Detective-Lieutenant Brady Baldwin, who tends to accumulate excessive fat around the belt buckle but none whatever between the ears. My relationship with Brady was good. Indeed, my relationship with all the city's official guardians was good. The reason, I think, was that we shared roughly the same brackets on the income-tax schedule. No class war where we were concerned.

"Hello, Brady," I said. "What brings you here?"

"Nothing brings me," he said. "Someone sent me."

"That's what comes from being discreet and efficient. You build a reputation. I've got a million references, Brady."

"Well, that wasn't quite the way this particular reference was. I've been talking with Mrs. Benedict Coon III."

"You can't please everybody. She didn't have to sic the cops on me, though. I offered to return most of the fee."

"I don't know anything about fees. Myself, I work on a salary. Someday I may get a pension. Invite me in, Percy. I've got a question or two."

"Sure. Come on in."

We went into the office, and Brady uncovered his naked skull and put the lid on a corner of my desk. He took a cigar out of the breast pocket of his coat, looked at it a moment and put it back.

"Mrs. Coon," he said, "gave you a job yesterday."

"The job was yesterday. She gave it to me the day before."

"Picking up her husband and a woman in the Normandy Lounge, and following them wherever they went."

"That was the job."

"She says you lost them."

"I didn't lose them. They lost me. No matter, though. The result was the same."

"Whichever way, it's too bad. You might have seen something interesting."

"I doubt it. You can't just invade privacy for something entertaining to look at."

"True. I'm glad you recognize your limitations, Percy. But murder, however entertaining, has no right to privacy."

"Murder!" I thought for a second that he was merely making an academic observation, but I should have known better. Brady wasn't given to them. "Are you telling me that he killed her?"

"Not he her. She him."

"Damn it, Brady, that doesn't figure. *She* was blackmailing *him*. Why the devil should she eliminate her source of income?"

"I've been asking myself that. There are a few good answers, when you stop to think about it. The best one, for my money, is based on the old chestnut that the worm sometimes turns. Say he'd decided to come clean, at whatever cost to himself, and to see that she got what was coming to her. It's not hard to find a motive there."

"If that were true, why did he meet her? Why didn't he call in the cops and be done with it once and for all?"

"Maybe he didn't make up his mind until the last minute. Worms do a lot of squirming on the hook, you know."

"Sure. So she shot him. Just like that. She had a gun in her purse, of course. Nothing odd in that. All women carry them."

"Not all. Some. Especially the ones who play around with blackmail. I wish you wouldn't indulge in sarcasm, Percy. It doesn't suit you. Besides, who said he was shot?"

"Didn't you?"

"I don't think so."

"I guess I might as well confess. I've read about murderers giving themselves away like this, but I never thought it would happen to me. The guilty knowledge was just too much for me."

"Oh, come off, Percy. It was a natural enough assumption. It's pretty obvious that she couldn't poison him in an automobile, and it would have taken an amazon to choke him to death. He wasn't any muscle man, but he could at least have fought off a woman."

"She could have stabbed him or cracked his skull."

"Maybe. But she didn't. She was carrying a .25 caliber gun, and she shot him with it—in the back of the head."

"That's crazy. What kind of man turns his back on a blackmailer?"

"He was careless, I guess. Why worry about figuring these things out, when you only have to ask. As soon as we find the woman, that is."

"You haven't found her yet?"

"We don't even know her full name, or what she

looks like. That's where you come in. Mrs. Coon says you can give us a description."

"That I can, and you couldn't be shot in the head by a choicer piece. Fairly tall. Custom built. None of your assembly line jobs. Pale blond hair, almost shoulder length. When I saw her, she was wearing a dark red suit with a skirt that showed off her legs, and they deserved it."

"Chassis can be disguised. Hair can be cut and dyed. It would be helpful if you had spent more time looking at her face."

"Have you been in the Normandy Lounge lately? I can tell you that it's just a little lighter than a cave. I tried to get a good look at her face, even in the mirror behind the bar, but all I can tell you is that it went well with the rest of her."

"You followed them, didn't you? It must have been lighter outside."

"As you say, I followed them. They were ahead, and I was behind. Would you care for an accurate and detailed description of her stern?"

"No thanks. I wouldn't want you to go poetic on me." Brady reached for his hat and slapped it on his head, a seasoned veteran of many a year. If the reference is ambiguous, take your choice. "Thanks for trying, Percy. Next time I've got a few minutes to waste, I'll look you up."

"Wait a minute, Brady. So maybe I blew the job. We all have our bad days. At least you can fill me in on what I missed. From what you said, I assume that Coon was shot in the car that he was driving."

"You assume right. It was parked on a dead-end road northeast of town. They'd apparently stopped there to wind up their business, whatever it was. Well, she wound it up, all right. Permanently. He was found early this morning, behind the wheel, with a hole in his head, slumped over against the door. It's really a county job, but we're lending a hand. Chances are, most of the investigation will have to be done in the city."

"Any leads at all on the woman?"

"Why, sure. You just gave us a couple. She's got

blond hair and pretty legs."

After which rather caustic remark, he heaved himself afoot and took himself off. I turned a hundred eighty degrees in my chair, looked into the alley, and wondered if it wouldn't be a good idea to jump out the window. With my luck, however, I would probably suffer no more than bruises and abrasions.

I'll not deny that I was feeling better. Somehow or other, my own fault or not, Benedict Coon III and his blonde charmer had spotted old Percy and played him for a chump, and Percy was hurt. He wanted to try again and do better.

Benedict was out of it, of course. He was lying in the morgue with a hole in his head. My job was done, or not done, and there was nothing left to do. Unless, perhaps, Dulce Coon would care to have me earn my fee by trying to find the elusive charmer who had killed her husband. That was, I thought, at least a possibility. I might not do any good, but chances were I wouldn't do any harm, either, and it was, after all, already paid for.

I decided that I would run out to 15 Corning Place and apply for the job. I put on my hat and went.

Corning Place was a long ellipse with an end cut off. The street entered at one side of the truncated end and came out the other side of the same end. In the center of the ellipse was a wide area of lush grass and evergreen shrubs, and here and there a stone bench. Outside the ellipse, forming an elegant perimeter, were the deep lawns and fancy houses of the people who could afford to live there.

Number fifteen was as fancy as any, two and a half stories of gray stone, with a wide portico protecting a section of the drive on the south end. I drove my clunker boldly up the drive and left it, without apology, under the portico. Farther back, I could see, the drive flared out in a wide concrete apron in front of a garage big enough for four cars below, and a servant or two in quarters above. I went up shallow steps from the portico and along a wide veranda to the front door. I rang and waited. Pretty soon the door was opened by a maid who asked me what I wanted.

"I'd like to see Mrs. Benedict Coon III," I said. "Mr. Percy Hand calling."

The maid was sorry, but Mrs. Benedict Coon III was seeing no one. She was lying down.

"It's very important," I said, exaggerating a little. "It's urgent that I see Mrs. Coon at once."

The maid hesitated, her expression indicating polite skepticism. It was evident that she had never seen anything important come wrapped in wilted worsted with frayed cuffs. There was always, however, an outside chance that I was legitimate. The maid finally said she would inquire, which was all the concession I could expect. I was permitted to stand in the hall with my hat in my hands while she went up a wide flight of stairs, elegantly curving, to make the inquiry.

The house was still. In the stillness, a stern citizen in oils looked down upon me with hard blue eyes. Benedict I or II, I guessed. I took two steps forward, and he was still looking at me. I backed up, and the eyes followed. Annoyed by my evasive maneuvers, the eyes were frigidly critical. The maid came down the stairs, fortunately, and rescued me.

Mrs. Coon had consented to see me. Would I please wait in the library?

I would, and I did, after the maid had shown me where it was. I waited in the midst of a dozen high windows, most of them draped, and several thousand shelved books, most of them, judging by their orderly arrangement against the walls, seldom or never read. A blond head appeared suddenly around the high, winged back of a chair near a window. The head was followed into view by a body, and they both belonged, head and body, to a young man wearing glasses, and holding a book folded over an index finger. With his free hand, the young man removed his glasses, and examined me curiously.

"Who are you?" he asked, as if he found me somehow incredible.

"Percy Hand," I said. "Mrs. Coon asked me to wait for her in here."

"Really? I didn't think Dulce was seeing anyone.

The police have been here, you know. They took her downtown to identify old Benny. A grim business. Very exhausting."

"I know. I won't disturb her very long."

"I wish you wouldn't. Dulce's taking it calmly enough, but you never know how close she may be to breaking. A remarkable woman, Dulce. You know what happened?"

"Yes. As you said, a grim business."

"Well, old Benny asked for it, I guess. He who dances and all that. Whoever would have dreamed that he was playing around? My name is Martin Farmer, by the way. I'm a kind of shirttail cousin. Remotely related."

I said I was glad to know him, which was a polite way of saying that I didn't give a damn one way or another. The hall door opened, and Dulce Coon came in. She was wearing a simple black dress and had slipped her feet into softsoled flats for comfort. Her dark hair, presumably just off the pillow, was still slightly tousled, as if she had done no more to repair it than comb it with her fingers. She didn't offer me her hand, but neither did she seem to hold a grudge.

"How are you, Mr. Hand?" she said. "Marty, what are you doing here? I thought you had gone out."

"I've been reading." Martin Farmer lifted the book, still marked at his place with an index finger, as evidence. "Are you feeling better, Dulce?"

"Somewhat. Don't worry about me, Marty. I'll be all right." She turned back to me. "I assume that you two have met."

"Yes, we have."

"In that case, what can I do for you? I thought that our business was ended."

"Not very satisfactorily, I'm afraid. I'm sorry."

"Don't be. One can't be called to account for every mistake. Did you come here just to apologize?"

"Partly. Not entirely."

"Why, then?"

"You paid me a large fee for something I didn't do. An excessive fee. If there's anything I can do, I'd like to earn it."

"There's nothing to be done. Nothing at all."

"This woman your husband was with. Myrna, you called her. I've been thinking that I might help to find her."

"Surely the police have far greater facilities for that than you have. Let the police find her."

"I have one advantage. I've seen her. I might recognize her if I saw her again."

"It's doubtful that you will see her again. It's probable that she has run away. If so, the police will follow her, or have her picked up and returned, if they can find her trail. I don't want to commit myself to anything that might interfere with their job."

"The police and I have worked together before."

"Please do as I say, Mr. Hand. I sent the police to you, and when you told them what you knew, you did all that was necessary. Now stay out of it."

"Right. Thanks, anyhow, for seeing me."

"Not at all. And now you must excuse me. I've had a difficult day, and I need to rest. Marty will show you out."

She turned away and left the room, and Marty, minding the manners of a shirttail cousin, showed me out. He said goodbye at the front door, and I crossed the veranda and got into my car. I drove forward to the concrete apron, U-turned and came back down the drive, around the ellipse, and out the exit.

On the way downtown I decided that I might as well spend some time, just for luck, in the Normandy Lounge. I went there and crawled onto a stool at the bar. I ordered a beer from the same bartender who had drawn my beer yesterday. A television set on a high shelf behind the bar was alight and alive with the organized antics of a couple of college football teams, reminding me that it was Saturday. The teams took turns trying to move the ball, but the only time they moved it very far was when they kicked it.

"Another beer," I said. The bartender drew it and served it. Bored by the game, his services temporarily unclaimed, he was ready for an ear to bend. Mine, being conspicuous, seemed to attract him.

"You been in the fight game?" he asked.

"Not I," I said. "Things are rough enough."

"Seems like I seen you before. A picture or something. Somewhere."

"Maybe it was yesterday. I was in here."

"Oh, sure. I knew I'd seen you somewhere. A guy don't forget a face like yours. You're no beauty, Mister. No offense meant."

"None taken. I guess it's true you remember the extremes. The uglies and the lovelies. Like that platinum-headed honey a couple of stools down."

"Where? What lovely? Mister, you're seeing things."

"Not now. Yesterday."

"Oh. That one. A doll. A sexpot. Plenty of class, though. You can always tell the ones with class."

"That's right. I could go for a woman like that. If I knew who she was I could work out a strategy."

"Mister, if you don't mind my saying so, you ain't exactly the type."

"You never know. Lots of lovelies go for uglies. You know her name?"

"Nix. We didn't introduce ourselves."

"She come in here often?"

"Never seen her before. Probably a guest in the hotel. Just someone passing through."

"How about the man she was with?"

"Was she with a man? I never noticed."

A customer down the bar held up his empty glass, and the bartender went to fill it. I helped myself to a handful of salted peanuts and left. Outside on the sidewalk, I ate the peanuts one by one while I tried to make up my mind if I should quit or give it one more try. One more try, I decided. Asking questions was a harmless diversion, unless I began to get some significant answers, and I had in mind the person to ask who would be most likely to have the answers.

I found her hunched over a typewriter in a blue fog, a cigarette, dripping smoke, hanging from a corner of her mouth. A pair of goggles was clinging to the end of her nose, and her red hair looked like it had recently been combed with an egg beater. She was wearing a sweater that fit her like a sweat shirt, and a skirt that she must have picked up at a rummage sale. I couldn't see her legs, but it was ten to one that her seams were crooked. It would be a mistake, however, to jump to any rash conclusion.

If you looked behind the goggles, you could see a face worth looking for. Inside the ragbag were a hundred and ten pounds of pleasant surprises. If you wonder how I knew, you are free to speculate. I will only say that she was a lovely, however disguised, who had no aversion to uglies. When she chose to make the effort, after hours, she could knock your eye out. Her name was Henrietta Savage, Hetty for short, and she wrote a column concerning things about town. You know the kind of stuff. Mostly about the fun spots, and who's doing what, where. It was innocuous enough, the kind of gossip that never goes to court, but in the process of gathering it Hetty had become a veritable morgue of interesting and enlightening items that had never seen print. She peered up at me over her goggles without appreciable enthusiasm, and the limp cigarette assumed a belligerent position.

"Don't bother to sit down, Percy," she said. "Go away. I'll meet you in the bar across the street after five."

"You're an avaricious female," I said. "How did you know I just got paid a fat fee?"

"Thanks for the confession. In that case, we'll have dinner later and a night on the town."

"Not unless you renovate yourself. I've got my reputation as a playboy to consider. Do you sleep in those clothes?"

"There's a possibility that you may find out. In the meanwhile, goodbye. Go away. Wait for me in the bar."

"I'm going, and I'll wait. Right after you answer a couple of questions for me. Come on, Hetty. Dinner and the town for a couple of answers?"

"Maybe lobster?"

"Pick him out of the tank yourself."

"What questions?"

"You know Benedict Coon III? That's just preliminary. It doesn't count."

"Your tense is wrong. He's dead. You'll find the

story on page one. Anyhow, I knew him, and make the next one count."

"All right. Who was the blond he was playing footsie with?"

"Benny? Playing footsie? Percy, you're libeling the dead."

"Not I. I believe in ghosts. I saw them together only yesterday, in the Normandy Lounge. Just barely, of course. You have to strike a match in that place to see your watch."

"You can buy a girl a drink without playing footsie. Maybe she was a cousin, or an old schoolmate or something."

"I have other evidence. From the best of sources. Never mind that, though. The thing is, I can't get any lead on her. I don't know who she is, or even how to start looking for her."

"Well, you won't learn from me. Who asked you to look?"

"No one, I'm just practicing."

"Go practice somewhere else. Damn it, Percy, I'm busy."

"Her first name was Myrna. That much I know."

"You know more than I. If there was another woman, I never saw her or heard of her. Benny must have been pretty cute about it."

"What sort of fellow was he?"

"Solid citizen. Something of a do-gooder. Bit of a prude, as a matter of fact, which helps to account for my skepticism. I can't quite imagine Benny among the primroses."

"Oh, can it. Hasn't anyone ever told you about the deacon and the soprano?"

"Tell me at dinner. Before you leave, however, here's something else that makes me scoff. Benny had been taking very good care of himself for the past year or so. Bum heart. Hospitalized after an attack. Strict diet, early to bed—the routine. Benny's hide was important to him. Gymnastics with a blond just doesn't fit."

"You never saw this blond. I did. The earlier to bed, the better."

"Blonds are deceptive. Anyone can tell you that red-heads are superior. Get lost, Percy. Go wait in the bar."

I thought it would be worth a lobster, so I went and waited, and it was.

Who was Myrna? What was she? A blackmailer, presumably. A spook, apparently.

Whoever and whatever she was, where in the devil had she gone, and where was she now? So far as I could discover, she had simply disappeared like a puff of smoke. No one knew her full name, no one knew her address, no one could remember her in association with Benedict Coon, and no one except me and a bartender could remember her at all. It was frustrating, it was uncanny, and moreover, it was incredible. A woman like that was a woman to remember. The bartender had said so, and I say so.

I was like a kid with a riddle in his head. I couldn't get it out, and I couldn't solve it. I worked at it when I didn't have something else to do, and I took it to bed with me at night, and I got nowhere from nothing.

Was it possible that Benedict Coon had killed her and disposed of her body, later killing himself in despair and fear and hopelessness? I was lying in bed when I had the thought, and it brought me straight up in the darkness. Then, jeering at myself silently, I lay down again. There is no suicide on record, so far as I know, who has shot himself in the back of the head and disposed of the gun afterward.

Perhaps the police had the answers. Perhaps, with all their facilities, they had gone somewhere while I was going nowhere. For the sake of my mental health, I decided to find out. The next day I went to police headquarters and found Brady Baldwin at a desk in a cubbyhole that may have covered a few more square feet than my reception room. If he was not exactly happy to see me, he was at least amiable.

"Sit down, Percy," he said. "What's on your mind?"

"Myrna," I said.

"Mine, too."

"You mean you haven't got any leads yet?"

"Not a one." He rubbed his naked skull and looked at me with an expression that was slightly sour. "As a matter of fact, I'm beginning to suspect that in your mind is the only place she ever was. How many martinis had you drunk, Percy?"

"I hadn't drunk any. I had a couple of beers. Brady, I saw her. She was there. She met Benedict Coon, and she left with him."

"All right, Percy, all right." He spread his hands and raised his brows. "But where is she now?"

"I was hoping you could tell me."

"I can't."

"You sure you've checked all possibilities?"

"All stations. Air, train, bus. Hotels, motels, apartment houses. The county boys have run all over the area trying to find someone who saw her walking, gave her a lift, anything at all. We can't go everywhere and check everything and ask everyone, but there's more. Shall I go on?"

"Sorry, Brady. I'm just frustrated. How far out was the car when it was found?"

"Not far; just far enough to put it in county jurisdiction. The state troopers are giving an assist out there. Benedict Coon, like I told you, was behind the wheel. Slumped against the door. His head had fallen forward. He hadn't bled much, a little seepage into his hair around the wound, that's all. This has been in the papers, Percy."

"I know. I just want it from you. When was he killed?"

"It must have been pretty soon after you lost them. The coroner says sometime between two and five. You know how those guys are. Try to box them into an hour, say, and they're slippery as a meteorologist. Thanks to you, we know that it was well after three. Probably past four."

"The paper said he was found by a real-estate agent."

"True. He happens to own the land beyond that dead-end road. He plans to push the road on through and finance an addition. He and a contractor had gone out to look the situation over."

"I can't quite locate the place. Where will the road come out when it's finished?"

"It won't actually come out anywhere. It'll dead-end again, against the rear of the Cedarvale Country Club golf course. The addition's projected for the upper brackets. As a matter of fact, Benedict Coon was a member of that club. Mrs. Coon was there the afternoon he was killed. She'd gone out to play golf with Martin Farmer, a family connection, and they stayed on for drinks and dinner in the bar. It was a clear day, you'll remember, after a rainy one."

"Is that where she was? I wondered. I tried to call her and couldn't get her."

"That's where. We checked it out just as a matter of routine. They were seen on the course and in the bar, and Farmer's car was seen in the parking area. It's a late model. There's a kid who works around the area, trimming the shrubs and controlling the litter, and he remembers the car particularly, because it had a full house."

"Full house?"

"Like in poker. On the license plate. This kid's sort of simple, and he amuses himself by trying to find the highest hand on the plates. Farmer's has three sixes and a pair of treys. It was his car, all right. Registry verifies it."

"Well, that's good work, neat and conclusive, but it doesn't get us any closer to Myrna."

"Forget Myrna, Percy. She's our problem. We're working on it, and we don't need you getting in the way."

"Thanks." Knowing when I'd been dismissed, I stood up to leave.

I went away, and with the help of several distractions I was able to keep Myrna pretty well confined to a dark closet at the back of my mind until that night when I was home in bed. Then she got out and began to make a nuisance of herself. I tried deliberately to think of someone else in her place, namely Hetty, but it didn't work. Lying on my back and staring up into the darkness, I let her prowl my mind without restrictions, and she began to repeat her performance in the

Normandy Lounge, the whole sequence of action; I saw her crawl onto the stool, saw her lift a martini glass toward a face that was a shadow in a dark mirror, and then, all at once she was walking swiftly across the hotel lobby beside Benedict Coon, and I could see the back of her. No more.

No more? Well, not quite. I could also hear her. I could hear the staccato rhythm of her spike heels on terrazzo, and I could hear at the same time, like an echo, a fainter, farther sound. Not another sound, but the same sound at a different time, and in a different place. The different time was a rainy afternoon not long ago, and the different place was the hall outside my office. There is a distinctive quality to the rhythm and cadence of a person's walk, if only you have the big sharp ears to pick it up, and I was ready to back my ears with odds that the person walking down the hall was the same person walking across the terrazzo floor.

Why? I asked myself the question with my breath caught in my throat and the short hair rising on the back of my neck. Why should Dulce Coon, wearing a blond wig and spike heels and Hollywood goggles and superimposed sex, meet her own husband in a downtown bar?

Well, that was easy enough to answer. Lots of wives met lots of husbands in various places for various reasons. As for the wig, women who could afford them were wearing them nowadays like hats. They changed hair with their mood and their dress.

What was more pertinent, why had she lied about a blackmailer who had probably never existed, and why had she deliberately arranged for a certain Percy Hand to witness a phony meeting in a shadowy lounge that had surely been carefully chosen for that reason?

That was a two-part question, and the answer to the first part was obvious even to me. She had simply wanted to plant a red herring, a blond bomb to divert suspicion from where it might otherwise have been directed. The answer to the second part was also clearly implied, and the implication was that Percy Hand, plying his trade in a side street with most of the trappings of failure and few of success, was a made-to-order sucker for a clever woman with murder on her mind. I didn't like the idea, but there it was, and it annoyed me considerably.

But wait a minute. Dulce Coon had been at the Cedarvale Country Club. She had been playing golf and drinking drinks and eating early dinner with her shirttail cousin. There were witnesses who said so, and the witnesses had satisfied Brady Baldwin, who was a hard man to satisfy. Could I be wrong? Had old Percy's big ears and little brain collaborated to lead him astray? Well, it was entirely possible. It had been done before. But still, lying there in bed and listening again to the sound of a woman walking, allowing for the differences in flats and spikes and wood and stone, I had a grim conviction that it was, in both times and places, no one but Dulce Coon.

Then another gorgeous idea bloomed all at once in my little hothouse brain. Not really an idea, though. It was more the remembrance of a minor observation that suddenly assumed a significant relationship to a scrap of information. Maybe it meant something, and maybe it didn't. But it brought me up and reaching out into darkness for the phone, and I dialed in darkness a number that I knew by heart and touch. At the other end of the line, another phone rang and rang, and I kept hanging on and on. Eventually a blurred and cranky voice broke in.

"Wrong number," the voice said. "Get off the line."

"Wait a minute, Hetty," I said. "Don't hang up."

"Who's this? It sounds like Percy, but I don't believe it."

"Percy's who."

"Damn it, Percy, it's almost three o'clock in the morning."

"Hetty, I just want to ask you a simple question."

"The answer is no. I'm too young, and you're too poor. It wouldn't work out."

"As you say. Now, will you answer my question?"

"You haven't asked it yet. How can I answer it if you won't ask it?"

"Here it is. What kind of heart trouble did Benedict Coon have?"

"How would I know? Is there more than one kind?"

"According to the best authorities, there are several. Could you find out for me?"

"If properly motivated."

"Bribed, you mean. What's the tariff?"

"Another dinner?"

"In the immediate future."

"Agreed. First thing in the morning. I've got connections at the hospital."

"Call me at my office."

"Just as soon as I know."

She hung up, and so did I. I smoked three cigarettes and lay down again. I was wide awake, and it was three years till daylight. There was another phone call I wanted to make, but I decided I'd better wait. Brady Baldwin, waked in the night, would be even meaner than Hetty, and he was not, moreover, susceptible to bribes.

The next morning I was in my office with my feet up when the phone rang, and Hetty was back. True to her word, motivated by a steak, she had found my answer, and it was the answer I wanted. Luck, after running bad, was beginning to run good. It looked like the end of a long, dry spell.

I dialed police headquarters. After preliminaries with the switchboard, I got Brady Baldwin in Homicide.

"Hello, Percy," he said. "No news."

"I called to give, not to receive. It's more blessed, supposedly. In brief, I've found her."

The line hummed, and I listened to it hum. Brady was still there at the other end, but he wasn't talking at the moment. I only hoped that I hadn't talked too soon and too much.

"Excuse me, Percy. We must have a bad connection. I thought you said you'd found her."

"I did, and I have."

"Where?"

"Sitting in my lap."

"Don't be a cutie, Percy. Give it to me straight and quick."

"Not now. Later."

"Better not play games with your license. You might lose it."

"No games, Brady. I could be wrong, and I have to be sure. Will you do me a favor?"

"Why should I?"

"You'll be doing one for yourself, too."

"That's different. What favor?"

"Do you still have Benedict Coon's car in custody?"

"We do, but we're ready to release it."

"What have you done to it?"

"The usual. We've taken photographs. We've lifted prints. We've vacuumed it and run tests. Nothing that's got us much of anywhere."

"Back seat, too?"

"Sure. We're not dummies, Percy. Coon was shot in the back of the head. It could have been done by a third party hiding on the floor in the rear. It's conceivable."

"How about the trunk?"

"Why waste time? How could he have been shot from the trunk?"

"Run tests on the trunk, Brady. That's the favor."

"Maybe you'd better come clean with whatever's in your mind."

"I said later, Brady, and that's when it'll have to be. Goodbye, now."

To avoid threats and recriminations and other forms of unpleasantry, I hung up, grabbed my hat, and got out of the office before he could call me back. I got in my clunker and headed east, and in due time I was rattling up the drive to the Cedarvale Country Club, which was not a place I ordinarily went or was welcome.

There were a dozen late vintage automobiles in the parking area. It was a clear day, chilly but still abnormally mild for the time of year, and I could see a few golf bugs scattered over the rolling course. In front of the clubhouse, using a pair of long-handled clippers on a juniper bush, was an angular specimen with an expression of contented idiocy on his face. He looked to me like the kind who might entertain himself by playing poker with license plates, so I wandered over and said that it was certainly a nice day, late in the year as it was, and he agreed. I said it was a good day for golf, and he didn't deny it. I asked him if a lot of members were still playing, and he said there were quite a few.

"You a member?" he asked.

"No, I'm a cop."

I didn't bother to distinguish between cops private, and cops public, and he didn't require me to make the distinction.

"There was a cop here the other day," he said. "He was asking about Mrs. Coon and Mr. Farmer."

"I know. You have to ask about things like that, just to keep the record straight. You know how it is with murder. It's important to find out where everyone was at certain times."

"Well, Mrs. Coon and Mr. Farmer were right here, and I said so."

"Did you see them?"

"Not them. His car. It was parked up here, and I remember it because it had a full house. Highest hand in the lot at the time. I play poker with myself, sort of, with license plates."

"So I've heard. Didn't you see them when they left?"

"They didn't leave. Not while I was here, I mean. Other people saw them, though. They came in off the course about four o'clock, something like that, and they hung around in the bar and had dinner before they left. I quit at five."

"When did they arrive and park the car?"

"I wouldn't exactly know. About eleven, I had to go down to the caretaker's shed for a tool I needed, and the car was here when I got back."

"How long did you stay at the caretaker's shed?"

"Well, I got to talking with a fellow there, and it was quite awhile. Half an hour, at least. A lot of other cars had come in, and the lot was pretty well filled. There was a luncheon in the clubhouse that day."

"I see. So the car was here soon after eleven, say.

Mrs. Coon and Farmer came off the course about four. I'd call that a long game of golf."

"They must have practiced before they started to play."

"That," I said, "is just what I'm thinking."

I left him in his juniper patch and went away. I should have gone directly to police headquarters, but I didn't, and the reason I didn't had something to do with earning a fee, and something more to do with injured pride or vanity or what you will. I went, instead, to 15 Corning Place, and I was intercepted at the door by the same maid as before, who went, as before, to see if Mrs. Coon would see me.

I waited in the hall for the maid to come back, but she didn't come. In her place, after awhile, Martin Farmer came, the shirttail cousin. He was superficially polite, but I could tell that I was considered a nuisance. Mrs. Coon, he said, wasn't seeing anyone. Mrs. Coon wasn't feeling well and couldn't be disturbed.

"That's too bad," I said. "Give my sympathy to Mrs. Coon, and tell her that Mr. Hand has important information that compels him to insist."

"Oh? Perhaps, if you were to tell me, I could relay the information to Mrs. Coon later."

It was a touchy point in our negotiations, and for a moment it seemed questionable whether I would get a concession or a polite bum's rush. Martin Farmer hesitated, considering the alternatives, then he shrugged and conceded.

"I'll see," he said. "Please wait in the library. You know the way."

I went to the library. I waited. After about five minutes had passed, Dulce Coon came into the library with her shirttail close behind her. Martin Farmer, that is. He stopped near the door. She came on and stopped a step or two away. This time she was wearing a white blouse and tight black pants. Her feet, bare, were thrust into flat sandals that were no more than thin soles with narrow straps attached. She was annoyed, to say the least, and she clearly was determined to make short work of me.

"Mr. Hand," she said, "I thought I made it clear that

our relationship had ended. Why have you come here again?"

"I'm here," I said, "to tell you that I've found Myrna. I thought you'd want to know."

There was a moment of silence in which no one moved or breathed. Then Martin Farmer stirred suddenly by the door, but I didn't look at him. I kept looking at Dulce Coon. Crimson spots had begun to burn in her cheeks, and her eyes glittered behind heavy lashes. Her lips moved soundlessly and were quickly still, as if she had been about to protest an impossible claim, Myrna being a myth. But this would have been a bad mistake, and she caught the mistake in time.

"Where?" she said.

"Where I least expected her."

"Don't be evasive, Mr. Hand. Who is she?"

"You. You're Myrna, Mrs. Coon."

"And you're insane." She laughed harshly, and her voice dripped scorn. "It's apparent that I made a mistake in coming to you in the first place."

"You made a mistake, all right, and your mistake was in taking me for more of a fool than I was. Once you had decided just how to kill your husband, you needed a witness to establish the existence of a murderess who didn't exist. Someone not very clever. Not nearly as clever as you, for example. I don't know just how you happened to pick on me, but I'm sorry that I couldn't accommodate you."

"Are you less of a fool than I thought? Clearly, you are even more of one."

"Let him talk, Dulce." The voice was Martin Farmer's, coming from the door, and it possessed a quality of silken amusement that warned me, suddenly, that I was listening to a dangerous man. "Even a fool can recognize foolishness if he hears enough of it."

"Thanks," I said. "I appreciate the opportunity to hang myself. Never mind how I finally tumbled to the fact that you were Myrna, Mrs. Coon. It took me long enough, and I'm not proud of it. Spike heels for added height, being careful at all other times to let me see you only in flats. A blond wig which can, incidentally, be traced, now that we know it was yours. Not only did it have to be bought, it also had to be dressed, and it will be only a matter of time until the police learn who sold it and who dressed it. For the big performance, a calculated emphasis of sex, which for you was easy. More than all this, dark glasses and a dark lounge and every precaution to prevent my getting a good look at you. Your face was always in shadows and turned away. When you left, you left quickly, exposing only your back in the light outside. Unfortunately for you, my ears are better than my eyes."

"What absurd thing is that supposed to mean?"

"Trade secret. I'll keep it, if you don't mind. Anyhow, once I knew it was you in the lounge, I could see that the whole show was phony. For example, you told me that you learned about Myrna by overhearing on an extension a conversation she had with your husband. In this house, there are surely several telephones, most of them without extensions. Why would your husband have received a call from a blackmailer on a phone which offered even the slightest opportunity for eavesdropping to a third person? I don't think he would have."

"This is really incredible. If it weren't so libelous, I might find it amusing." Her voice was still harsh, however soft, and the blood still burned in her cheeks. She was possessed, I thought, by a kind of unholy excitement. "Now that you have decided that I devised this elaborate hoax, perhaps you will tell me why I wanted to murder my husband."

"You tell me. Money? That was part of it, I suspect. Money, and the man who helped you murder him."

"So now there is a man involved. What man, please?"

"The man you met in the Normandy Lounge. Martin Farmer."

"This is getting more and more absurd. You *are* insane, aren't you? I thought all the time that I was presumed to have met my husband there."

"That's what I was expected to presume, that the man in the lounge was your husband. But he wasn't. He was Martin Farmer. Your shirttail cousin. His term, not mine. He had only to exercise the same care that you did to get away with it. Wear the clothes you said your husband would wear. Keep his face obscured in the shadows. He has about the height, the right weight, the right color hair. Everything but the right name and the wife."

"But my husband was murdered. Remember? Where, exactly does he fit in?"

"He fits in the trunk. The gray sedan's trunk. He was killed here, in this house, sometime around two o'clock in the afternoon, late enough to satisfy the estimate of time of death, which allowed considerable latitude. After losing me in the traffic, you drove out, put him behind the wheel, and left him where he was later found."

"You're ignoring something, aren't you?" It was Martin Farmer again, and I turned to look at him. There was an air of indolence about him, and he was smiling faintly, but his eyes were cold and wary. "Dulce and I were at the Country Club. We played golf and had drinks and dinner. We were seen by a dozen people who remember."

"No." I shook my head and began to wonder, now that I was almost finished, if I could ever get out alive. "Your alibi is the most precarious bit of all. To have a car handy, you drove your car out to the club before noon and left it in the parking area. But you didn't stay. I imagine that Mrs. Coon followed you and brought you back here, where you had work to do, having arranged in advance for the necessary privacy in which to do it. You know the work I mean. Your golf bags were put into the sedan, along with a change of clothing. After parking Coon's car on that dead-end road, it was a simple matter to change, and pack into the golf bags that you carried away with you the clothes you removed. It was only a matter of minutes to cross that undeveloped land between the end of the road and the back of the golf course. Risky, of course, but you were ready to take the risk, and you made it. Then you came on into the clubhouse, a pair of innocent golfers with a car to ride home in, and witnesses to testify for you. But I can't remember anyone's saying that you were seen before coming off the course.

It was simply assumed that you had been playing. Brady Baldwin's a smart cop, and he'll be interested in that."

"This is very interesting speculation," Dulce Coon said. "Even rather clever. I advise you, however, not to repeat it. It's actionable, you know, and you would have to account to my lawyer."

"I predict that you will have to account to a lawyer yourself. The prosecuting attorney, I mean. Don't forget that the gray sedan is still in custody. The police lab is working over the trunk right now, and you can lay odds that they'll find something to show that your husband took a ride in it—a thread, a scraping of skin, a hair or two, a smear of blood, something. It's miraculous, the things that can be done in labs these days. Brady will be along after awhile. You can depend on it. In the meanwhile, since you brought your lawyer into this, I'd recommend calling him early."

I had started moving toward the door, and I kept on moving, and no one tried to stop me. I slipped past the shirttail cousin and out and away.

At least, I thought, I had finally earned my fee.

At dinner, we were three. I was there, and Hetty was there, and Brady Baldwin was there. Brady was included because he had finished the case and earned a dinner, and because I was feeling expansive. Three assorted fiddles and a piano made music, and it was, altogether, very fancy and satisfying. After dinner, Brady's ulcer began to bother him a little.

"I've got to go home and take something," he said, "and so I'd better humor you immediately and have it over with. I'll admit you acted practically like a genius in this business, once you got going, but there's one thing that must have been pure boneheaded luck, a wild guess, at best. How did you tumble to the fact that it was Martin Farmer that Dulce Coon met in that bar? Maybe it wasn't even a guess, though. Maybe, when you met Farmer later, you simply recognized him."

"Nothing of the sort. Brady, don't try to belittle me. There was a strong resemblance between Farmer and Coon, and I never got a good enough look to see any difference. Farmer saw to it that I didn't. So far as I knew, it was Benedict Coon at the bar, and Benedict Coon who left with his wife. It was only later that I learned something that convinced me that it was really someone else. Under the circumstances, the shirttail cousin, being suspiciously handy, was indicated."

"All right, I'll bite. What did you learn?"

"Thanks to Hetty, I learned that Benedict Coon had a serious heart condition. Not that he couldn't have lived for a long time, too long to suit our Dulce, apparently. Especially since, according to reports, he stuck strictly to his diet and took damn good care of himself."

"Come off it, Percy. You can't tell that a man has heart trouble just by looking at him. You trying to tell me that the man at the bar looked like he *didn't* have heart trouble?"

"It wasn't how he looked. It was what he did. Hetty checked it out for me, and she reported that Benedict Coon's specific heart condition was something called cardiorenal disease. People who have it are put on a very strict salt-free diet. And the man at the bar, all the time he was waiting, kept eating salted peanuts."

Hetty was drinking coffee and smoking a cigarette, and looking at me through the smoke with a very promising expression.

"Isn't he remarkable? You said it yourself, Brady. Practically a genius, you said. It makes me all over prickly just to know him."

"Well, I'll be damned." Brady shoved back his chair and stood up and looked down at me sourly. "Good night, Hetty. Good night, Genius. Thanks for the dinner. I'm going home to bed."

"In good time," said Hetty, "so are we."

THE COMPLEAT SECRETARY

Theodore Mathieson

Three hundred miles south of Portland, Oregon, over the mountains, Dunbar's four-passenger plane ran into stormy weather, and his compass started acting erratically. Minutes later his engine misfired, then went dead, and as he dived below the clouds to find a landing spot, he found the plane skimming the pinetops of a hillside forest.

In the back seat, his wife Emma let out a wail. "Oh, Howard, look at the snow! It must be ten feet deep down there—and all those *trees!*"

"Do you think you can crash-land?" Hallie asked in a steady voice.

He glanced at his attractive secretary, and their eyes met and locked momentarily. "We're going to have to try."

"Oh, Howard, we could get hurt!" cried Emma.

"If you can think of any other way, let me know. Just check your belts and hold on."

Already the crowns were almost scraping the belly of the plane as Dunbar picked out a spot ahead where the trees seemed thinner and younger. Pulling up slightly on the stick, he began to pray.

Dunbar's head struck an overhead brace just as the tearing and ripping began, and with splintering noises the plane settled into the young pines. In the rear he could hear his wife whimpering, but his first concern was for Hallie. She looked shaken, and held her hand to her face, but she still sat upright.

"I think Emma is hurt," she said practically.

As he started to move, pain shot through his wrenched body, but he decided no bones were broken. Managing to open the door of the plane, he stepped down the two or three feet to the ground. Snow lay all about, perhaps a foot deep, but the air was warmer than he'd expected and, under the larger pines, circular patches of needles lay high and dry.

"We'd better stretch Emma out in one of those dry spots," he said, and reached into the plane to unstrap his wife's seat belt.

He felt Hallie's hand upon his, and her voice sounded strange. "Don't you think you ought to be sure about her back before you move her?"

"I'll handle her all right," he said, more roughly than he'd intended. Lifting Emma in his arms, he carried her up the hill from the plane.

She was still moaning, her eyes closed, as he laid her down on the needles. She seemed to be scarcely conscious, but she was in one piece, and there was no bleeding. He went back to the plane to get a blanket.

"Well?" Hallie asked. She hadn't moved from her seat.

"You can't tell if there's anything really wrong with her yet. She'll have to come to, first."

Once again Hallie's hand touched him. "You better cover her," she whispered.

The enormity of the invitation at such a time set Dunbar's legs trembling as he carried the blanket up the hill and tucked it around Emma. He stood for a moment looking down at her.

Then he hurried back to the plane . . .

"We could be together all the time, Howard. Nobody would know."

Hallie's last whispered words kept running through Dunbar's head as the three of them sat under the pine tree and she bandaged Emma's broken ankle with a piece of lining torn from the plane's interior. Leave it to Hallie to do everything efficiently. Before becoming private secretary to Dunbar, president of Dunbar Electronics, Inc., she'd been a registered nurse, and had brought her meticulous skill to managing Dunbar's peripheral affairs. He'd never known her to make a mistake. Even on a business trip, interrupted now by the accident, he'd taken Hallie. She was indispensable as well as decorative, in spite of an eye that had been blackened by the crash. He'd only brought Emma along out of obligation.

His wife, conscious now, screwed up her pallid, middle-aged face and let out a yelp of pain.

"Catch hold of yourself, Emma," Hallie said firmly. "You're lucky the three of us are *alive*."

"I know," Emma said, sobbing. "It's just that I could never stand pain."

When she'd had Robbie, their only child who had died when he was three, Emma had screamed the hospital down. The only endurance she'd ever shown, Dunbar reflected, was in sticking to him long after even habit had palled.

Nobody would know.

Avoiding Hallie's eye, Dunbar moved back to the plane and looked at the sky, filled with low, dark clouds. It was close to dusk, and there was the feel of snow in the air.

The planes from Redding, where he'd planned an overnight stop on their way to Las Vegas, would be out looking for them in a little while. Unfortunately, he'd put off installing a radar device in the plane, so they'd have a tough time spotting him in this wilderness, if indeed they could find him at all with the ceiling so low.

Still, he'd better start gathering some chaparral, soak it with gasoline, and keep the fire going all night. He walked over to a dead bush and then stopped.

Do I want them to find us so soon?

He glanced up the hill and saw that Hallie was watching him.

"There are plenty of blankets in the plane," she called down, as if she read his thoughts. "We could be quite comfortable for tonight. It's not very cold, and tomorrow you could go for help."

"Yes, I guess that would be the better idea." It was just as if he sat behind his desk in Portland, and she were advising him on the agenda.

Around midnight it began to snow lightly. Hallie sat in the seat next to Dunbar, while Emma lay stretched out in back. Her whimpering, which had gone on for hours, keeping them all awake, had subsided now and she snored deeply and regularly.

"Have you thought about it?" Hallie whispered, pressing his thigh with intimate urgency.

He looked at Hallie in the faint snowlight which filtered into the cabin. What a queen she would make for the king of Dunbar Electronics! Not only was Hallie knowledgeable in all his business affairs, but she had *style*—and passion, too, behind that efficient exterior.

"Yes, I've thought," he said finally.

"Well?"

"I could never do it, Hallie."

"Would you like for me to take care of it?"

"I . . . don't . . . know."

She did not reply, and they continued sitting in the half light, intensely aware of one another. Instead of becoming sleepy, Dunbar found himself keyed up, the way he was before a crucial board meeting. Then, as a faint light appeared in the east, he made his decision and felt better for it. Although he didn't say anything, Hallie seemed to sense the moment that he'd come to it . . .

After the three had breakfast of some chocolate bars, washed down with tepid tea from a Thermos, Dunbar got out of the plane and made a big pile of dead chaparral in a clearing on the hillside, soaking it with gasoline.

"Keep an ear out for the planes, Hallie," he said, "and if you hear any, light up at once. I'll try to find a main road."

"May I have some of your matches?"

For the first time that morning their eyes met, and there was perfect understanding. He knew Hallie had matches in her purse with her cigarettes.

"Yes, of course," he said, giving her a folder. "Don't lose them, now."

"I won't."

"Now you be careful, Howard," Emma warned from inside the plane. She wriggled out on the seat so her skinny legs in their slacks hung over the fuselage. "And remember, we don't have much to eat back here."

"Well, I don't either. I'll do my best."

"We'll all do our best," Hallie said.

"Yes, I'm sure you will."

He looked at Hallie, the way he always did when a course of action had been decided on at the office, and gave her a curt nod. *The go-ahead.*

Then he turned and plodded off down the hill.

Dunbar was no stranger to the woods. As a boy he'd roamed the Sierra Nevadas, following the trails and exploring the twistings of remote creeks. He knew his first task was to find a logging road, if that were possible, preferably one that led upward, for the sooner he could get to a ridge and a wide view, the better. The slopes above the plane had been too steep and craggy to climb.

At first he was so busy plodding through the drifts that he had little time to think. But as he descended, the snow thinned and walking became easier, so that more and more his mind dwelt upon what lay behind him rather than what lay ahead.

Emma hadn't been a bad mate, she just had never been a *wife.* For twenty years he'd shelved any hope of freeing himself, able to submit to the status quo only by cultivating outside interests. Not until Hallie had come along last year, however, had the thought of breaking away been so strong, filling him with such a wild hope for freedom that he wondered how he could have stood his marital imprisonment.

When he suggested divorce to Emma, she had shrieking hysterics, then tried to commit suicide. She threatened, too, to tell things she knew about certain foreign deals, which would surely blacken his name in this country. So he'd given up, which satisfied Emma. If she knew about Hallie, she didn't show it. Sometimes Dunbar suspected Emma was a little feebleminded.

He heard the plane after he'd been walking for an hour or two. It was flying low, and he caught sight of it skimming above the trees. In an instant of thoughtlessness he almost ran into a nearby clearing and waved, but then he stood still, keeping his face down.

After a few seconds, he climbed up on an outcropping of rock and looked back the way he'd come. No sign of smoke was visible.

Hadn't Hallie taken care of the matter yet?

Meanwhile, the plane had droned away to the south-west without circling, so apparently the wreck had not been sighted.

Walking again, Dunbar began to worry. What if their failure to contact the rescue parties immediately resulted in their not being found? Main roads were pretty scarce in this region, and he could walk for days. All he had with him was a bar of chocolate and some water in a cola bottle, and Hallie didn't have much more.

On impulse he almost started back to warn her, so they might all get out alive, but then he remembered that since Hallie never procrastinated on the job, it was probably too late.

Around noontime he came upon the trace of an old logging road that led him for hours over open timber-land until finally, as daylight began to fade, it petered out amid an open stand of ponderosas.

He stood now in the meadow, which was dry and free of snow, listening to the lonely thud of his own heart, feeling sure that Emma was going to have the last, hysterical laugh, and they would all die together.

Then he heard the engine of a car close by.

A few steps farther on, he saw the highway lying just below him at the bottom of a steep cut, and as he descended to the road the lights of a car appeared upon a distant curve.

By the time the car got close enough for him to see the two occupants in the front seat, he was standing on the shoulder, waving like mad.

Then an inner warning, out of nowhere it seemed, hit him like a thunderbolt.

Instantly he was running ahead of the car, beyond the cut, to where the hill curved down to a creek. He dived into the underbrush and cowered like a truant kid. The car stopped close by, he heard the door open and the murmur of voices, then the door slammed and the car went on.

Dunbar crouched for a long time at the bottom of the ravine, spent and shivering, realizing how near he'd come to bringing disaster upon himself and Hallie. He cursed himself for not thinking of it sooner. It was pure habit for him to leave details to Hallie's judgment, but this was one time he should have done more thinking himself, and his failure to do it might still cost them their lives!

It was early next morning when Dunbar staggered wearily back to the wreck. Hallie was sitting on a stump in her tailored overcoat, working on a fingernail with a file. There was no sign of Emma.

She ran to him and put her arms around him. "Couldn't you find a road? One plane flew over yesterday morning, and two in the afternoon . . . but I wasn't ready."

Dunbar took a ragged breath. "Did you do it?"

"Of course."

"Where is she?"

"Now, don't worry. Everything's under control."

"Look, I found the highway. It's about four or five hours' walk over that way, so we'll get out—but we'd better wait. Just as I was flagging down a car, I thought about—well, if she was supposed to be killed in the wreck day before yesterday, she'd be cold, or have rigor or something. Rescue guys could get here in a jeep in just a few minutes, and if they found her still warm—"

"I told you not to worry, dear," Hallie said, pointing to a long mound of snow up the hill a ways.

"You mean—"

"She's been in there since yesterday. I think we should take her out now."

"My God, Hallie . . ."

His secretary went up to the mound and began scooping away the snow.

"What took you so long, darling, if it's only a four-hour walk?" she asked.

"I lost my way coming back and had to spend the night around a camp fire." He turned away as he saw the pink blanket in which Emma was wrapped. "H-how did you do it?"

"I'd like to spare you the details."

"I'd like to know."

"The only feasible way. Her neck was broken in the crash, naturally."

"She didn't suffer?"

"Of course not. I put her out first with pressure on the carotid artery."

"That was merciful."

"You can carry her back to the plane now. This blanket isn't even wet."

He laid Emma out in the back seat, and then Hallie said, "I think we'd better light that bonfire. There'll be more planes, won't there? Oh, and one more thing. Those people who stopped are bound to be curious about why you ducked out, and the story might get around."

"We'll say I was delirious with hunger and exhaustion, and was suddenly afraid they were going to run me down."

"Then you blacked out from that bump on your head," Hallie said thoughtfully, "lost the road, and ended up back here. It might do in a pinch, but maybe we'd better start the fire, and you can go back to the highway."

The sheriff and two deputies arrived just as Dunbar got the chaparral blazing.

"The people in that car were mighty puzzled," the sheriff said, when Dunbar had made his explanations, "but your blackout reaction is understandable under the circumstances, and it's lucky they reported it. You've been mighty fortunate, Mister Dunbar, and you, too, Miss. Sorry I can't say the same about Missus Dunbar."

The deputies carried Emma's body on a litter down the hill to a back road that Dunbar had missed, and loaded it onto a jeep. Then the sheriff drove Dunbar and Hallie in his car into town, where the executive and his secretary checked into a hotel.

"Telegraph a cancellation to the meeting in Las

Vegas," Dunbar told Hallie over a lunch of filet mignon and Burgundy, "and I'll go make arrangements with the undertaker. We'll ship Emma back to Portland."

"When will we be married?" Hallie wanted to know.

"Five, six months."

"Are you pleased with me?"

"Perfectly, as always."

She gave him a professional little smile.

It was while Dunbar was at the mortuary late that afternoon, that the sheriff came in and asked him to go with him to the courthouse.

"Just a few routine questions, Mister Dunbar," the sheriff said respectfully.

But when the door had closed behind them, and Dunbar sat facing the sheriff across the desk, the latter's eye became anything but respectful.

"What I'd really like to know, Mister Dunbar," he said, "is which one of you killed your wife—you or your secretary?"

"I'm afraid I don't understand."

"Oh, yes, you do. That story about getting delirious doesn't work, when you think about it. We followed your tracks to where you built a camp fire; that took recollectedness, I figure, and then you didn't go back to the road for help. You say you were lost, but were you?"

"I don't have to answer your questions," Dunbar countered.

"Also, I noticed that the blanket that was around Missus Dunbar was sopping wet. Guess that one of you didn't know much about snow, thought it was dry in the cold air. You evidently didn't realize that powdered snow can feel dry outside, and melt at a higher temperature, like inside the plane's cabin. We went back to the area of the wreck, you know, and found where she'd been buried."

"To keep the body cold, yes. We didn't know how long we'd be there."

"It's too late for subterfuge, Mister Dunbar. We've already got a complete confession from your secretary in which she admits being an accessory to the murder. She says *you* broke your wife's neck, trying to make it look like an accident, just before you went off for help—"

"Oh, no, you don't!" Dunbar cut in. "Hallie—Miss Cross, is not likely to confess things which neither of us did."

The sheriff pushed some typewritten sheets across to Dunbar. On the last page he recognized Hallie's signature, and when he scanned the typescript, he knew the sheriff wasn't bluffing.

"It's a lie!" he shouted. *"She* did it. She talked me into letting her do it! Then, when I was on the road, I became suddenly afraid that if you found us right away, you'd also find that her—my wife's—body was still warm, when she was supposed to have died the evening before."

"That's why you went back, as I figured," the sheriff said.

"But I might have known," Dunbar said bitterly. "Hallie never made mistakes. It was I who put Emma into the plane with the snow-covered blanket around her."

"If she really killed your wife, Mister Dunbar, she made one, too. As a matter of fact, I might have accepted the whole story as you told it except for *that* mistake."

"What was it?" Dunbar asked, in disbelief.

"If your wife had died in the crash with a broken neck, at the same time as she undoubtedly broke her ankle, would either of you have bothered to tape up the ankle with the torn lining from the plane's cabin? The bandage, Mister Dunbar, was still around her ankle."

THE HYPOTHETICAL ARSONIST

Rog Phillips

"What makes you think this man set fire to your building when the fire department is so positive it was not arson at all?" Justin asked the man who leaned over his desk, being too impatient to sit down.

The name on the business card the man had given Justin was *Reginald Hall,* and his business as stated on that card was *Financial Investments*. He was almost a foot taller than Justin would be if he stood up. He had practically forced his way past Miss Higgins in the outer office with the forceful aggressiveness of a brigadier general.

"Nothing, sir," the man said. "Nothing at all—except a form of instinct. He submitted a bid for rebuilding too soon, and it was too accurate. It strikes me as odd."

"Why not take it to the police or the fire department?" Justin said. "Why come to me?"

"In my leisure I have been a hunter," Reginald Hall said, leaning with his hands flat on the desk while Justin blinked up at him owlishly through his thick-lensed glasses. "When one senses a dangerous animal in the bushes, one does not get a pack of baying hounds. Besides, one whisper from my direction and I could be sued. The sign on your door says *Justice, Incorporated*. I have noticed the sign many times. Auditors, Incorporated, handle my business records and they are just down the hall, you know."

"Yes, I know," Justin said, neglecting to tell Reginald that he also owned Auditors—and Private Eye, and most of the businesses on this floor of the building. "There is also an outfit called Private Eye, Incorporated, on this floor. Why didn't you talk to them? As private investigators, your suspicions would not go beyond them, I'm sure."

"I'm aware of that, sir," Reggy said. "If there were a single shred a private detective could work from I would be tempted. But why beat around the bush? I admit the name on your offices intrigued me. Justice, Incorporated, Justin P. Lord—almost as though you were Divine Providence come down to Earth to smoke out the rascals the law can't touch. It appealed to me, sir."

"Sit down and tell me about this man you suspect is an arsonist," Justin said, taking out a carved cigarette holder and inserting a cigarette in it.

"Thank you," Reggy said, sitting down and accepting one of Justin's cigarettes. "His name is Walter Moore. He is in his fifties, is a thoroughly respected and competent building contractor with a D and B top rating, engages in new construction much more than reconstruction, and most certainly doesn't need the money. I can't imagine what possible motive he might have had for setting fire to my rather shabby old office building, unless it might be to provide work for one of his crews until a legitimate job comes along. Would that be possible?"

"You own the building at Market and Elm?" Justin asked. "The one that had a fire last week, in which three people died?"

"Yes," Reggy admitted. "One of them was an old and wonderful friend. I think if I could be absolutely positive in my own mind that Mr. Moore started that fire I would not bother with you, but would kill him with my own hands."

"I doubt that," Justin said. "Still, you have come to the right place. If he's guilty, I'll smoke him out."

"How much?" Reggy asked bluntly, taking out his checkbook.

"I'm tempted to do it free, Mr. Hall," Justin replied. "However, I have expenses. How much can you afford? Five thousand? Ten?"

Reggy scribbled a check, ripped it from the checkbook, and let it fall on the desk under Justin's gaze. It was made out for ten thousand, which proved that Reggy did have an instinct, the right one, at that.

The moment Reginald Hall left the office, Justin punched the phone button for the extension in Private Eye, Inc.

"A man just left my office," he said. "Huge, a dynamo, named Reginald Hall. Have him followed, report often. I want to be sure about him, even though I think he's all right. When you get that going, send in the research team. I want someone investigated back to his birth."

Next, Justin punched the button on the phone connecting him to Auditors, Inc.

"Do you have the accounts of Reginald Hall?" he asked. "You do? How much is he worth? Almost a millionaire? So ten thousand wouldn't bother him at all."

"He asked us about Justice, Incorporated," the man at the other end said. "We told him what you have instructed us to say when we are asked, that it is a nonprofit organization which uses rather unorthodox methods to bring justice, both to the guilty the law can't touch, and to innocent victims the law can't help. We prepared him by telling him if he had a problem you would accept, you would be very expensive because he could afford it, but for someone who is poor you would work just as eagerly for free."

"Are you handling anything concerning his burned office building?" Justin asked.

"The whole thing. He will come out quite well on it. The contractor, Moore Construction, submitted a bid just below the figure the insurance company quoted as the maximum they will pay. He will actually have a better building. However, one of those who died in the fire was a lawyer who was a long-time friend of Reggy's, though not his legal counsel. His name was Arthur Brand. He had apparently been working late, and was trapped by the flames."

"You like Reggy?" Justin queried.

"Oh, yes, he's one of the best, though a trifle dynamic and impatient. His wife, Helen, is a wonderful woman with a quiet sense of humor; does some translating into English from French nonfiction works. My wife and I have been to dinner at their house."

"Thank you, Marvin," Justin said. After he hung up he sat motionless, frowning in thought, until Miss Higgins ushered in the research team from Private Eye. Like all the employees of Private Eye, they bore no noticeable or unusual characteristics.

"The man I want researched," Justin said, his eyes blinking slowly behind his thick-lensed glasses, "is Walter Moore, the building contractor. It's possible he may, secretly and for much of his life, have been a compulsive arsonist. He must not know he is being investigated, in case he is innocent. I want you to find out especially if his home burned down when he was a child. It would be an indication. Also look into his first beginnings as a building contractor. See if you can find any seeming coincidences of his getting the contracts to rebuild structures damaged by fire. He is probably married and has children, who may have grown up and left home. He may have brothers and sisters. Find out. I want a quick job. Don't check with police or insurance companies unless you first find direct evidence that he has been arrested somewhere, sometime. I doubt that he has ever even been suspected of arson. I doubt that anything could be proved against him. If I am wrong, and he stands a chance of being tried and convicted in court, we are out of the thing until and unless he is tried and declared not guilty. Then I come back in, in my own way. Now get busy. He is in the phone book, and you know your business."

When the research team had left, Justin, as an afterthought, punched the phone button to Auditors, Inc., again.

"Do you have Walter Moore, Moore Construction, or Moore Contractors as a client?" he asked. Then, "I didn't think so. No, it's just as well you don't. I would rather he didn't notice the existence of this building."

Finally, Justin rang for Miss Higgins and handed her the check.

"Photostat this and hold up depositing it until I say to," Justin said. "It always pays to be suspicious of any client I don't go out and get myself, in this business.

He is a client of Auditors, though. Start a file from theirs, Miss Higgins."

"Yes, Mr. Lord. What cross-classification should this account be under?"

"Arsonists," Justin said, "Hypothetical."

"Who?" Miss Higgins asked. "Reginald Hall?"

"It's a thought," Justin said. "I mustn't overlook that possibility, but no, he's our client. The name for the secret file is Walter Moore. It should be quite a busy file for the next two or three days."

Reginald Hall, at breakfast in his shingle-siding house that had been built around the turn of the century, was angry at himself. He was often angry with himself at breakfast. His wife Helen would have begun to worry about him if he weren't, two mornings out of three. It was, she realized, part of his energy, his drive. Perhaps it was what had made her fall in love with him when he first courted her many years ago.

"I must have been out of my mind to give that man ten thousand dollars!" Reggy said, buttering his toast viciously. "What do I expect him to do? Murder Mr. Moore? Subconsciously I must expect that! My instincts again! I have a nose for things, and my nose sniffed a professional killer there; but I like this Justin P. Lord, damn it!"

"Then he isn't a professional killer, Reggy," Helen said with quiet assurance. "You could not like a murderer even if you didn't suspect he had ever killed someone."

"But this Justice, Incorporated, business!" Reggy said. "What else could it be? Administering justice to criminals the law can't touch! Indeed! *That's* what made me pay him ten thousand dollars."

"I would like to meet Mr. Lord," Helen said. "You seldom like a person so immediately and so violently."

Reginald gaped at his wife, then continued eating his breakfast.

"It's been three days," he said. "I'm going to his office this morning and jack him up or demand my money back. Besides, I forgot to ask him, should I let Mr. Moore rebuild my building? I wish I didn't have it in my head that Mr. Moore started the fire. I'm sure he didn't. I don't know what gave me the idea. Sometimes I think I would be better off with a psychiatrist."

"Now, Reggy!" Helen said in alarm. "I shudder to think what a bore you would be."

Reggy snorted. "I would, wouldn't I?"

In better humor he continued his breakfast, and later he caught Justin in his office. Part of his annoyance toward Justin P. Lord was that he had been unable to get anywhere with figuring the man out. Mr. Lord, aside from his owlishly magnified brown eyes, was a very mild appearing man who could be married to a shapeless wife with ten children, and who was in this business of *Justice* in order to escape from his responsibilities at home—or he could be a bachelor who lived in a hotel room and whose whole life centered around his business activities. It was impossible to tell. The man had a loose skin, like he might have once been quite fat and his skin hadn't shrunk when he lost the fat. His features reminded Reggy of the face of a bloodhound, a little, although Mr. Lord's habitual expression was not the deep sadness of the bloodhound's expression but instead bordered on the intellectual scowl.

"What have you been doing?" Reggy came straight to the point.

"Things are moving," Justin said with a shrug.

"Have you seen Mr. Moore?"

"I've seen several candid camera shots of him taken by one of my men without Moore's awareness."

"What do you think of him?" Reggy asked.

Justin shrugged without answering.

"Of course," Reggy said. "What I really came to see you about was, should I go ahead and let him rebuild? What should I do?"

"Hmm," Justin said. He inserted a cigarette in his holder and lit it before answering. "If you give him the go-ahead, and he is an arsonist, he will undoubtedly retreat into being all business and avoid further direct contact with you. Delays in making decisions are normal when there has been a fire and repairs must be made. On the off chance that I might decide on some

move that would necessitate your inviting Moore somewhere, he would be more inclined to accept if he still
thought the contract depended on it."

When the time was auspicious, Justin summoned
Reggy and Mrs. Hall to his office.

"What do you want us to do?" Reggy asked.

"You must have a dinner party at your house and
invite Walter Moore and his wife. If he hesitates about
coming, drop a hint that you will make a definite decision on the building contract that evening."

"All right," Reggy agreed. "Who else do I invite?"

"I'll give you the list," Justin said. "I will be one of
them. Is this Friday evening too short notice for you,
Mrs. Hall?"

"Not for me," Helen said. "What do you plan on
doing? Expose Mr. Moore?"

"And open us both to suit for slander?" Justin said.
"I don't work that way!"

"How do you work?" Reggy asked with frank blunt-
ness.

"Complexly, Mr. Hall," Justin said, "and yet, not
too mysteriously. People are very much like molecular
substances. They react or don't react in any situation
according to their properties. A chemist creates a situation where a substance will react the way he wishes it
to; I create a situation where a person will react the
way I wish him to. Get Mr. and Mrs. Moore to come
to your house at seven, Friday evening. My people will
be there at six, so that we can be ready."

"How many shall I expect?" Helen asked.

"Just be ready," Justin said. "A caterer will handle
the refreshments and straighten things up afterwards so
that you won't have to do a thing except be the most
charming hostess." Justin smiled at her, then shifted his
smile to Reggy. "A contriver? That I would have never
suspected!"

It was a very nice party, Helen decided when dinner
was served; nice, except for the florid Mr. Ardmore
who talked too loudly, and Mrs. duVres who was
rather ludicrous with her mink stole and her insistence

on wearing it even while eating. Mr. duVres was a nice old gentleman though. And there were so many people, over twenty. Mr. Lord was posing as a traveling lecturer and humanitarian who had come with the duVreses, and possessed the suavity to portray the part.

Mr. Moore and his nice wife, Erna, hadn't the slightest suspicion that it was all set up for them. Mr. Moore was rather impatient to get the go-ahead on the contract, and neither he nor his wife were really enjoying themselves, but they were resigned to the evening and to Reggy's promise that he would make his decision soon.

"Justin P. Lord?" Mr. Ardmore spoke up suddenly. "I've heard of you. Friend of mine heard you lecture back east once on—what was it?—the criminal who is never caught? Isn't that a contradiction? No one is a criminal until he's caught, ha ha!"

"If you say so, Mr. Ardmore," Justin answered with an expression of distaste.

"No, come now," Mr. Ardmore chided. *If you say so,* is that any way to answer a man? Is there or is there not a criminal who has never been caught?"

"There probably is," Justin said. "If he is never caught or even suspected, and he dies and his criminal acts are never found out, no one will ever know he is a criminal. Nevertheless, he is one. Rare, perhaps—or more common than we think."

"Wasn't there a woman who poisoned fourteen successive husbands before she was exposed?" Mrs. duVres gushed. "Isn't it possible there are women who have equaled her accomplishment and never been smoked out?"

"It's possible," Justin said. "In fact, it's well known that many murderers are never caught, but also most murderers don't keep on murdering. They do it once, then stop. In my lecture I was talking about the habitual criminal who can't stop, but is never caught. He is more interesting because in the field of crime he chooses he can never make a mistake, and he keeps increasing the odds against himself by being unable to quit. I chose an arsonist for my hypothetical criminal because arson has so many potentialities, and is a recognized form of mental illness."

"But then he would be a sick person, not a criminal," Mrs. duVres said.

"No, I don't think so," Justin responded. "He would be ill only in the sense that a one-armed man is. Remember, he has never been caught. He has learned to live with his compulsion and to compensate for it. No one notices it, or will ever have the slightest reason to suspect him. In fact, there are so many ways a compulsive arsonist will eventually be caught that we can predict quite accurately what he will be like by the time he is, say, fifty years old—assuming he exists."

"You mean," Mr. Ardmore snorted, "any who aren't like him will already have been caught before they are fifty?"

"Yes," Justin said. "But first of all, how did he get started? Like all arsonists. He set his first fire when he was perhaps eight years old. He was home alone, there was a pile of wrapping paper in a room that hadn't been cleaned up. On impulse, he got a match and started the fire. There was the excitement of the bright red fire trucks, the few weeks of living somewhere else, then the excitement of moving back into a rebuilt home, with no one thinking to ask him if he set the fire. Rewards, rewards, rewards. Also cautions. The insurance man saying to his father, 'Good thing you never had a fire before. Next time won't be quite so easy!' and his father saying, 'Don't worry, we'll never leave a pile of paper laying around again,' and both of them laughing, secure in the knowledge of their lack of guilt."

Justin paused to put a fresh cigarette in his holder and light it. Helen and Reggy saw Walter and Erna Moore dart a swift, uneasy glance at each other, then look back toward Justin.

"It had to be that way," Justin said. "Those first-timers who set fire to something other than their own home did not get a lesson in the future hazards an arsonist will inevitably face. This one did. Eventually he set his second fire, perhaps not until he was twelve or older, and his third fire and his fourth. There was the first fire in which someone died. It was a horrible shock but he got over it. His schoolmates at about this age were getting over their first feeling of remorse at having shot a rabbit or a bird.

"But he never set fire to his own home again. He was determined never to get caught, and he was developing all the thousand and one instincts that would prevent him from even being suspected during the rest of his life. The rest of his life? Yes, *he can't quit!*"

Justin said this with firm emphasis and looked directly into Walter Moore's eyes, then let his gaze pass on to others so that Walter Moore couldn't be sure it had been purposeful.

"By the time our arsonist was twenty," Justin went on, "he was developing a philosophy that would normalize his periodic compulsion to set fires. What sort of philosophy? One that would partition that part of his life from the rest, like a cancer? No, one that would *embrace* his compulsion. How? In two ways: by concentrating on the good that stems from the tragedy of fire, and by building his career on that good. He had a choice of careers that fit this formula. Bright red fire engines are nice but abnormal. The insurance man was, he sensed, an enemy. But the carpenters were friends, and they were *builders*. So, perhaps even during high school, our arsonist became a carpenter. Later, he became a building contractor. When jobs slacked off he picked out houses to set fire to, to damage a porch, or one room, just to give him a small job. By this time he was an expert and stood little chance of ever being caught, but two hazards still lay ahead of him. One of them was a wife, who would get to know him better than anyone should. He had to marry and have a family, of course, because he had to remain normal or eventually he would make a mistake.

"So at the age of fifty he is married, has raised a family, has grown children, who don't live at home, and *his wife knows his secret*. She discovered it, of course, somewhere along the way, could not turn him in, and gradually learned to accept it, though never as an active partner in arson. She began to believe in the good that came out of fire; the slum buildings that were destroyed, then replaced by new buildings; the stricter enforcement of safety ordinances that saved more lives than were lost in the fires her husband set; the money her husband made when he got a big contract to rebuild what he had destroyed. . . ."

Justin blinked slowly, looking directly at Mrs. Moore, but not seeming to do so intentionally.

"There would almost have to be a church," Justin went on. "A minister who wanted the old church torn down and a new one built, and a congregation that thought the old church was good enough. A fire would solve that. A new and more beautiful church would rise from the ashes, a spirit of brotherhood would grow in the congregation as funds were raised—and there would, of course, be the new preacher to replace the old one who died of a heart attack brought on by the fire. There is always so much *good* that comes from tragedy."

"Then what is the second hazard?" Mr. Ardmore asked. "It seems to me he will never be caught. His wife keeps out of it, and by now wouldn't want him to quit. What else could trip him up?"

"His inability to quit," Justin said. "Oh, he has been and will always be extremely careful, and under ordinary circumstances he could continue setting fires until he dies of old age. In his contracting business he doesn't rely on arson to make more work. On the contrary, most of his work is new construction, most of the time he doesn't even bother to get the contract for rebuilding what he has burned down. He doesn't need the business.

"No, the final hazard he can never avoid, and which is always there," Justin said, "is that someone, sometime, will get an illogical—almost a psychic—*hunch*. Of course, no one will ever be able to prove anything that has already happened in the past. The house he was born in burned down when he was eight, but that proves nothing. A neighborhood church burned down when he was thirty-three, but he and his family weren't even members of that church. What can be proved?"

Helen and Reggy were watching with fascination the change coming over Mr. and Mrs. Moore. They had grown very pale, and didn't seem to be breathing at all as they stared in horrible fascination at Justin Lord.

"No," Justin said, shrugging indifferently. "Nothing out of the past can trip up our arsonist. But if he is singled out and some expert organization keeps him under observation, twenty-four hours a day, week after week, month after month, sooner or later he will have to set *that last fire,* the one that convicts him, because he will be seen in the act, photographed in the act, caught in the act, arrested in the act, and by that time he won't care. He will be desperate beyond desperation, he will, at last, be truly *sick!* He has tried to keep from setting fires and he can't. He can't—any more than any of you could stop breathing by an effort of will and hold your resolve not to breathe until you were dead. He has to set *one more fire.*

"He will know he is followed," Justin said, "but eventually he will convince himself he is not. He will know those who know about him, know they are right about him, but eventually he will convince himself they had no idea he exists, and were just talking about a hypothetical person."

This was Reggy's cue.

"Well, all of this is very interesting, Mr. Lord," he said. "You are an excellent public speaker. I'm delighted that the duVreses could bring you to our party, but methinks you are a compulsive speaker."

"I admit it, I admit it!" Justin said. "I apologize and will shut up, provided I am properly rewarded with another of your fine drinks."

"I'll get you one right away," Reggy said, hurrying toward the kitchen.

Walter Moore gave his wife a warning look and hurried after Reggy, catching up to him in the kitchen.

"We'll have to be going," he said. "About that contract—"

"Do you have it with you?" Reggy asked. "I'll sign it right now, if you have."

"I don't—" Walter Moore said, then halted himself by an obvious effort of will. "Yes, I have it." He took it out of his inside pocket.

Reggy laid it on the corner of a table and signed it, glancing up with a smile.

"You're a contractor!" he said. "What beautiful sophistry that makes. All successful arsonists who reach their fifties are building contractors."

"My crew will start Monday," Walter said, smiling. He turned abruptly and left the kitchen.

Reggy opened the kitchen door far enough to watch. Walter Moore went to his wife, and then both went to Helen to say good night and leave.

Reggy finished making the drink, wondering how Justin Lord's little speech was going to affect Walter Moore and his wife Erna. That *hypothetical* business was strictly phony, of course. Mr. Lord had been quoting historical facts he had uncovered. And Mr. Moore, the contractor, would know that. He would know beyond any doubt, by now, that Mr. Lord was pretty sure he was an arsonist.

But would that make him go to the police and confess? Reggy doubted it. Also, he doubted very much that twenty-four hour surveillance of Moore would work. Why, he himself could think of half a dozen ways to set a fire while being constantly watched. Fires that wouldn't start until hours or days later! And he was far from an expert!

Reggy returned to the front of the house and delivered Lord's drink. There seemed to be some sort of argument going on, but he made no attempt to catch the thread of it until he had rejoined Helen.

"Not all of you can take part in it," Mr. Lord was saying. "You should have enough sense to see that."

"I think I should take part, Justin," Mrs. duVres was answering, almost angrily. "After all, it's been years and years!"

"What's going on?" Reggy whispered to Helen when he sat down beside her.

"You'll never guess!" Helen whispered back, positively titillated and quivering with excitement. "Listen . . ."

"I think I should have his house!" Mr. Ardmore said. "I'm a charter member!"

"All by yourself?" several voices protested.

"I see our host is confused," Justin said. "Mr. Hall, I should explain. In my discussion of the successful arsonist, I neglected to say anything about the ones who, somewhere along the line, get caught. What happens to them? They are, of course, confined, in prisons and state mental institutions, but eventually they have paid for their deeds or appear to have recovered sufficiently to be returned to society. What then? They face much the same problem as the alcoholic who has been dried out in a prison or state hospital. The only way their compulsion can be controlled is by banding together into a society of their own kind, to help one another fight that impulse—or if not fight it, to direct it into a constructive channel."

"You mean," Reggy said in sudden amazed comprehension, "these people are—why the initials are the same, aren't they!—Arsonists Anonymous?"

"You're darned right!" the florid Mr. Ardmore said. "And I want the right to set fire to Mr. Moore's house!"

"You see, Mr. Hall," Justin said, shrugging sadly, "the group has become imbued with the desire to recruit Walter Moore. One of the inflexible rules of A.A. is that only the property of a practicing arsonist is fair game, and they are hungry, starved for action."

"Yes, indeed," Mrs. duVres said, smiling at Reggy with something bordering on pride. "I was recruited this way. It was so wonderful discovering there are people who really understand, who have been through it themselves, and who have banded together to help one another. Why, Mr. Hall, you have no idea how many hours we will spend preventing one another from setting fire to YOUR house, now that we have seen it. But have no fear, your house is perfectly safe, because we all know that if it did burn, we would have a session and find out who did it."

"A pity, too," Mr. Ardmore said. "That nice shingle siding, and dry as tinder. But let's get back to the business at hand. Mr. Lord, I leave it to you, shouldn't I get to burn Walter Moore's house?"

"Don't be so eager," Justin said. "After all, he has enough property for all. His contracting company offices and sheds, the fifty houses under construction in his housing development, but it all must be done slowly so that the insurance companies will cancel his insurance. You must all use self-restraint."

WHO WILL MISS ARTHUR?

Ed Lacy

Swallowing hard as I studied Velma stretched out beside me, I could only think: does murder start as simply, as matter-of-factly, as this? In hundreds of other crummy hotel rooms, people were having affairs, but was any other lover staring at his woman, his mind full of killing?

I've never bothered figuring exactly what it is Velma has for me, but she has it all the way. She's hardly the most beautiful woman, nor the cleverest, but there is a kind of wistful, childish charm about her, a dash of pure pixie innocence. Even in small talk Velma has a refreshing naivety. Could be her appeal is the obvious: both of my ex-wives had been take-charge, sophisticated, worldly women.

I knew what I was going to do, yet it seemed absolutely unreal. How was it possible for a middle-aged and cynical joker like myself, a man with his own small ad agency and a comfortable income, to say, "Velma, we have to kill Arthur!"

The words sounded hollow in the quiet hotel room, not because I had any feelings about her creepy husband, but only because I'd never thought of murder before in my life. Yet I'd mouthed the words and I'd meant them!

Velma sat up, slim, cute, wide-eyed, as if waiting for the punch line to some poor joke. "Come on, Frank, why so mad? Okay, Artie's taking me to Nassau for a week's cruise and you and I won't see each other next week. But this—wild talk, I don't like it even as a gag."

"Honey, it isn't a gag and I'm not talking wildly. I've weighed every word. Velma, can't you understand that

I'm fed up with this backstreet romance bit? I want you for myself, for all time. Bullheaded Artie won't give you a divorce, and you tell me things won't work out if you just leave him, so . . ."

"Frankie, darling, don't be angry with me. I really know Arthur and his bookkeeper's mind, narrow as an adding machine. Unfortunately, I'm on the credit side, if that's the correct term, where he lists his assets, and if I walked out on Arthur, he'd follow us, crawling and wailing, spoiling life for us. We couldn't be happy. Darling, if only I'd met you first!" Velma snuggled against me, and I felt the soft warmth of her smooth skin.

Gently pushing her away, I said, "Honey, let's face up to some facts. We love each other. Arthur won't budge, so he has to be removed. It's that simple."

"In time we'll work out something and . . ."

"Pure bunk! I've been selling myself that line for the last five months. Not a thing will change in time. It has to be *now!*"

"But, Frankie, merely because he's taking me on a cruise? You never talked of . . . of killing before. How can you say it so calmly?"

"Baby, do I sound calm? I'm not, I'm all nerves. Honey, I'm neither a criminal nor a violent type, but when you leave me, the thought of Arthur touching you . . . well, if I ever meet him on the street, I don't know what I'll do. This cruise provides a foolproof means of knocking Artie off."

"But, sweet, you know how the cruise came up? After Artie turned down my plea for a divorce, without alimony, he suggested the cruise and it's the first time in our six, lousy, married years he's ever got off a dime. The cruise won't change me and, if it will make you happier, I won't go. But please, stop talking about . . . murder."

"Velma, I want you to go on the cruise, it's our only out. Otherwise, I'll explode one of these days, beat Arthur to death, and end up in jail! Velma, I know what I'm doing, believe me."

"Oh, Frankie, I do believe you. But how c-can a cruise mean a safe way of k-killing Artie?"

I poked my finger at her cute pug nose. "Baby, do you recall how we first met?"

She giggled nervously. "How can I forget? I saw you on the street and, from the rear, thought you were Arthur. I went boldly up to you and made a fool of—"

"Because I'm the same height, weight, age as your hubby, look a little like the dope. Velma, listen carefully: cruise ships generally dock here Saturday morning, unload passengers, take on supplies, then sail again in the afternoon for another week's cruise. Your ship is due to sail at 6 p.m., meaning it will already be dark. I want you to take your time, stall, don't board the ship with Arthur until after 5 p.m. You'll go to your cabin where the steward will have a fast look at Mr. and Mrs. Arthur Harper. The steward has other cabins to handle, plus seeing a steady stream of different passengers all spring and summer. Now, I'll board the ship, as a visitor, at 5 p.m. Nobody will stop me, or ask my name. When all the other drunken visitors have gone ashore, I'll remain on deck. The stewards will be busy, will assume I'm a passenger. By 7 p.m. the ship will be well out on the Atlantic. The other passengers will be in their cabins, unpacking, sobering up, getting ready for dinner. It's now very dark and—"

"I still understand. What's all this to do with . . . us?"

"I'm coming to that, Velma. All you have to do is insist on Arthur going to the stern of the ship with you, for a last look at the shore lights, or you have a headache. He'll do that. I come up, hit him on the neck, throw him over. We're already a dozen miles at sea, so his body will never be found. Then you and I, as Mr. and Mrs. Arthur Harper, return to our cabin and dress for dinner. Simple?"

There was a moment of heavy silence in the cheap hotel room, Velma giving me a childish, big-eyed stare. "But your luggage, Frank?"

"I'll wear Arthur's clothes, we're the same size. We enjoy the cruise and the following Saturday, when the ship docks in New York again, Mr. and Mrs. Harper walk off. No passports are involved. Immigration will be a mere formality. Honey, I've been on these cruises before, and I know the procedure."

"After we leave the boat, then what, Frankie?"

"Nothing. We go directly to my place and start living there as Mr. and Mrs. Frank Preston. Keep your office job or toss it over, whatever you like. In time, we'll get legally married, but the main thing is, all the time we'll be living together, no more of this sneaking around. Arthur has no friends or family, who's going to miss him?"

Shivering slightly, Velma leaned against my chest. "Frank, can it actually be so easy, no risk?"

"Baby, the only risk is that his corpse might come ashore, but the odds are in our favor. Yes, there's another risk, somebody *might* see us in the brace of seconds it takes to toss Arthur over. But on these cruises, the first few hours after departure people are in their cabins, unpacking, resting from the going-away shindigs. As for my handling Artie, a chop on the neck and over he goes; a few seconds of danger rewarded by our lifetime together." I listened to my own voice, like an outsider, amazed at my calm manner, as if I killed a man any old day. I didn't tell Velma the *real* risk, whether I could go through with a murder. But I despised sniveling Artie so deeply, wanted Velma so badly, I felt I could do it. The . . .

Velma shook me. "Frankie, didn't you hear what I asked?"

"I'm sorry, honey. What did you say?"

"I asked if the cabin steward wouldn't notice that you're not Arthur?"

"Darling, passengers are a blur to a steward and he'll only get a fleeting glimpse of Arthur when you first go to your cabin. Sure, you, a redheaded dish, he'll probably remember, but when he sees you and a man of Arthur's stature return to the cabin to dress, why should he doubt they are Mr. and Mrs. Harper? If you mistook me for Arthur, he surely will. Baby, all we have to do is play things cool and we're set."

Velma shivered like a little girl frightened by a bad dream. "Oh, Frankie. Frankie, I'm scared!"

I held her tightly. "So am I, hon, I'm almost hysterical. But a few rough seconds and we're together forever. Velma, it's the only way. I just can't take this anymore, and beating Arthur to death in a street brawl isn't any answer. Darling, all you have to do is have him at the ship's stern at 7 p.m."

Things broke our way. It was drizzling when the liner left the Narrows and rocked out into the ocean, so the dark deck was empty. Artie wore a new, tan trench coat and when I slugged him on the neck, I propped him against the rail for a second, removed the trench coat and his wallet. He went over like a sack, vanishing instantly into the wake of the propeller. I tossed my coat over and put on the trench coat, then grabbed Velma for a moment, to keep her from screaming, or maybe to keep myself from yelling. I kept whispering, "Velma, it's *done! Done! Done!*"

She nodded, her face blank with shock. I shook her. "Baby, snap out of it. We've made it."

"Yes, yes. Listen, can I have a drink?"

"Sure, but just one. Let's go."

That was the first and last show of nerves we had. We walked back to *our* cabin. I took the key from Arthur's coat pocket, unlocked the door. When I rang for the steward and ordered drinks, he said, "Yes, sir, Mr. Harper." After he left, Velma and I stared at each other . . . and laughed, too loudly.

I didn't shake as I opened Arthur's bag, hung up his (my) things. Velma opened her suitcase and also a smaller bag she had for toilet articles. I found a well-wrapped package in 'my' bag, which I tossed to Velma. She said it was a gift Arthur had mentioned buying her. I examined the wallet. He really had meant to live it up, had $563 in cash. I had plenty of cash on me, but I'd purposely left my wallet and papers ashore.

Velma and I had a few drinks, ate dinner casually, danced, returned to the cabin and slept soundly, to my surprise. The next morning was sunny and we relaxed in deck chairs. I was wearing a new pair of walking shorts Arthur had bought in some bargain basement, and Artie's sport shoes, which fitted fine. At the Captain's Dinner that night, Arthur's tux was hardly in the best style, but it made me appear an old married type.

Oddly, there wasn't a single moment of remorse for

either of us. Velma had difficulty remembering to call me Arthur, but solved that by calling me "honey." We truly had a ball on the ship. Tuesday morning we docked at Nassau and as we were about to leave for Paradise Beach, the steward told me I was wanted in the purser's office. The purser asked mildly, "Are you and Mrs. Harper leaving us today, sir?"

"The ship is our hotel in port, isn't it?" I asked, tense.

"Mr. Harper, surely you remember buying only a one-way ticket for you and your wife? You told our city office you'd leave the ship here, island hop, then return by plane."

"Oh yes," I said quickly, "but I thought my secretary had informed your office about changing our minds. That girl—I don't know why I keep her. Anyway, we decided against the island hopping. Can we keep our cabin and return with the ship?"

"We're delighted you're staying with us. That will be an additional $330 in passage. We'll take a check, if you wish, Mr. Harper."

"I'll pay it in cash, leaving less money for the wife to waste in the Straw Market."

When I returned to our cabin, I had to keep my anger under wraps. "Velma, why the hell didn't you tell me you and—that we were to leave the ship here?"

Her sweet face was so startled I knew she wasn't lying when she said, "Leave the ship? Why do that? When Ar—you first mentioned the cruise, I was told to ask for a week's leave. I mean . . . I don't get this."

I dug the tickets from an inside coat pocket, which I suppose I should have done at once. Sure enough, they were for a one-way passage. Showing them to Velma, I told her, "It doesn't matter now, but I think —*somebody* was going to stay here, or island hop and return later by jet, although I don't see any plane tickets and five hundred bucks isn't much for that kind of touring. Honey, think back carefully." I dropped my voice to a whisper. "Are you certain he didn't mention leaving the ship here?"

"No, no. I was to ask at the office for a week's leave and he was doing the same at his. A second honeymoon, he called it. He wasn't the talkative kind, which was one reason he bored the heck out of me, but after I asked for the divorce and made a scene when he refused, why—he said he had this surprise for me. We'd go on a cruise, that he realized I didn't have much fun in life, all that pleading jazz. I told him it wouldn't change my mind, but agreed to take the week's cruise since he already had the tickets."

"Well, let's forget it and start for the beach. I guess, with $500, he could have spent a few days in the islands, then used a credit card for the plane ride back to New York. Let's go."

We rode a glass-bottomed boat to Paradise Beach and had a great time. Velma was a redheaded dream in a bikini, her slim body already a fine tan. Oiling her skin, I warned her to be careful of the tropical sun. We left the beach at 3 p.m. and took a boat back to the main street, where Velma bought the usual straw bag and hat and a few souvenirs. It was hot, and we returned to the ship to dine in air conditioned comfort, then went on the nightclub tour, sweating through Limbo dances, rum, and the usual tourist routine.

The following morning we swam at Paradise Beach again, then stopped at the post office where Velma sent a few cards to the girls in her office. I didn't send any cards; I was supposedly fishing "someplace" on the Cape. I grinned as I thought how well I was keeping in Arthur's character; he'd be too cheap to waste money on postal cards. By 4 p.m. we were on the ship, tossing coins to the native divers while waiting for the liner to depart.

The two-day voyage back to New York was restful. We danced, played bingo, slept a lot, and were very happy. I had murdered and really didn't feel a thing, except thankfulness that Velma would be mine from now on.

The night before we were due to dock, I filled out our Customs forms. We were each well within our duty free limit but Velma seemed a little nervous. "Honey, in the morning, all we do is walk off the ship?"

"Almost. Tonight we put our bags outside the door so they can be taken up on deck. Saturday morning, while the bags are being put ashore, we line up for Immigration; we'll be asked if we're citizens, and that's all. If necessary, I'll show Arthur's credit card for identification, and you'll show them your office ID. Then we get our landing cards and leave the ship. Customs men wait for us on the pier, we show them what we've bought, and we leave."

"That sounds simple. Honey, how about that bottle of perfume Ar—you bought me? Should I declare that? I've never even opened the box."

"No. If Customs insists on seeing it, doesn't believe it was bought here, we're still under our limit. Customs won't be any problem; we're not smugglers."

Saturday morning was clear and after an early breakfast we watched the liner go slowly up the New York Harbor. Velma was still a bit tense, but Immigration was a snap. Our landing cards were stamped and as we started down the gangplank, me carrying Velma's small toilet bag, she whispered, "Will the Customs people search us? Undress us, like on TV?"

"Stop being silly. Velma, show them the things we've declared, all in the straw bag you're carrying. They may run a hand through our bags and that will be the ball game."

Velma handed me Arthur's gift package. "Honey, I . . . what will I do about this?"

"Baby, stop shaking. I told you, *if* asked, explain it was given to you here, last Saturday, before sailing. If they think it was bought in Nassau, why, you add it to our declaration."

"Frank, it *isn't* perfume!"

"Dammit, watch what you call me!" I whispered. "What's in the package, Velma?" I hefted it in my hand; it was not very heavy.

"I—well—I tore off one side of the paper wrapping a little while ago, curious as to the brand of perfume it was and . . . Honey, look at it!"

Turning the little package over to the torn side, I abruptly stopped walking down the gangplank. What I saw was green—a thick green stack of twenty dollar bills!

People behind us called out to keep moving. Slipping

the package into my trench coat pocket, I took
Velma's arm, gripped it. "Where did this come from?"

"I don't know! I merely tore part of the wrapping off
and—Oh, Fr—honey, what do we do?"

I stared at Velma. She gave me her helpless, child-
like look of despair. She whispered, "I swear, I never
knew he—he had money. Darling, what do we do?"

I forced a grin. "Relax and forget it, act natural. I'll
keep it in my pocket for now, open it while we're waiting for Customs, spread the money around my pockets,
no bulge. Velma, it's okay, the odds are the Customs
men won't look in my pockets and . . ."

We'd walked off the gangplank. Now, two large men
blocked our way. I knew they were police before one
of them flashed his shield, asked, "Mr. Arthur Harper?"

"Yes. What's all this about?" I asked sharply, and as
I said the words, at that split second . . . How clearly
it came to me!

The other detective shook his meaty head in amazement. "You must be some kind of a nut. You steal
$50,000 from your boss and then have the nerve to re-
turn to New York . . ."

ARBITER OF UNCERTAINTIES

Edward Hoch

Arthur Urah was a tall, slender man with thick white hair and the bearing of a dignitary. He wore silk shirts with the monogram *AU* over the left breast pocket, and this was what had led some in the business to dub him the Arbiter of Uncertainties. It was a good name. It fit him perfectly.

He had never been to the Brenten Hotel before. It was in an old section of town, and in truth it was an old hotel, dating back some fifty-five years in the city's history. No one of importance stayed at the Brenten any longer, and thus it was perhaps a bit odd to see a man of Arthur Urah's obvious character entering the lobby on a Sunday afternoon.

"I'm to meet some people here," he told the desk clerk, a seedy little man chewing on a toothpick. "My name is Arthur Urah."

"Oh, sure! Room 735. They're waiting for you."

"Thank you," he said, and entered the ancient elevator for the ascent to the seventh floor.

The corridors of the old hotel were flaky with dead paint, and a dusty fire hose hung limply in a metal wall rack. Arthur Urah eyed it all with some distaste as he searched out room 735 and knocked lightly on the door.

It was opened almost at once by a slim young man with black hair and pouting lips. Arthur Urah had known the type for most of his life. The room itself was as shabby as the rest of the hotel, and its big double bed had been pushed against one drab wall to give more floor space, revealing in the process a long accumulation of dust and grime.

"Arthur! Good to see you again!" The man who

came forward to greet him first was Tommy Same, a familiar figure around town.

Arthur Urah had always liked Tommy, though personal feelings never entered into his decisions. "How are you, Tommy? How's the family?"

"Fine. Just fine! Glad to have you deciding things, Arthur."

Urah smiled. "I don't play favorites, Tommy. I listen to both sides."

The other side was there, too. Fritz Rimer was a little man with a bald head and large, frightened eyes. It was obvious at once that he was out of his league. "Pleased to meet you, Mr. Urah," he mumbled. "Hate to get you down here like this on a Sunday."

"That's his job!" Tommy Same pointed out. "You and me've got a disagreement, and Arthur here is going to settle it. He's an arbiter, just like business and the unions use."

Arthur Urah motioned toward the door. "I'm not used to settling cases with a gun at my back. Get rid of the kid."

Tommy Same spread his hands in a gesture of innocence. "You know Benny. His father used to drive for me. Benny's no kid gunman."

Urah eyed the slim young man with obvious distaste. "Get rid of him," he repeated. "Let him wait in the hall."

Tommy made a motion and Benny disappeared out the door. "Satisfied?"

Urah gave a slight nod, running his fingers through the thick white hair over one ear. "Now, who else is here?"

"Only Sal. She won't bother us."

Urah walked to the connecting door and opened it. Sally Vogt was lounging in a chair with a tabloid newspaper. "Hello, Arthur," she said. "Just catching up on the news."

He closed the door. "All right," he decided. "She can stay. Nobody else, though. Tell the room clerk nobody comes up till we're finished."

"I told him that already."

Arthur Urah opened the slim briefcase he carried

and extracted a notepad. "We'll sit at this table," he said. "Since Fritz is the offended party, he gets to talk first."

It was only an outsize card table, with rickety legs, supplied by the hotel. Sitting around it on their three chairs, they looked a bit like reluctant poker players defeated by the odds.

Fritz Rimer cleared his throat and nervously fingered a pencil. "Well, everybody knows what the trouble is." He paused, as if suddenly aware of his smallness at the table.

"Suppose you tell us anyway," Urah prodded gently.

"There are thirty-six horse rooms in this city where a man can lay a bet on the races or the pro games. Twenty years ago, when I started in business, there were thirty-six individual owners of these places. We all knew each other, and helped each other out. When the cops closed down one place occasionally, the rest of us came to the owner's aid. We were one big family, see?"

Tommy Same moved restlessly in his chair. "I'm crying for you, Fritz. Get to the point."

"Well, about a year ago, Tommy Same and some of his syndicate friends moved in and started taking over the city's entire bookmaking operation. Some places they forced out of business and then bought up cheap. Others, they demanded a big cut of the take and sent somebody around to baby-sit and make sure they got it. Right now the syndicate is a partner in thirty-five of the thirty-six places in this city—all but mine."

Arthur Urah nodded. "And now he wants yours, too?"

"Right! He sent that guy Benny down last week to scare me, but I told him this wasn't like the old days. I don't scare. If he wants to kill me, he can, but that just might be the end of Tommy Same." As he talked, a certain courage seemed to flow into the little bald man. Now his cheeks were flushed and there was an unmistakable power in his words. The others had not stood up to Tommy, but little Fritz Rimer had, even though it might cost him his life.

Tommy Same cleared his throat. "When do I get a

chance to talk? You going to listen to this guy all afternoon?"

Urah smiled slightly. "You can talk now, Tommy. Is Fritz telling the truth? Are you trying to take over his operation?"

Tommy Same leaned back in his chair, frowning. "It's like labor unions, Arthur. We all have to stick together, to protect ourselves from the law, and deadbeats, and occasional swindlers. With all thirty-six horse rooms in town linked together in a sort of syndicate, it's better for everyone."

"And that's your defense for this?"

"Sure. I'm not trying to force anyone out of business. I'm giving valuable services, and I just want a share of their profits in return."

"Did you threaten Fritz here?"

"Look, this isn't the old days! If I'd threatened him, do you think I would have allowed him to call you in? Do you think Capone or some of the other old-timers would have sat still for arbitration?"

"You're not Capone," Arthur Urah reminded him quietly.

"No, but I can realize the importance of us all sticking together! If Rimer goes his own way, pretty soon the others will start to, and then where'll we be? Back to the old days when the cops could knock off the places one at a time."

It went on like that for another hour, with each man arguing for his side. Arthur Urah had heard it all before, in a dozen different contexts, and at these times the dialogue took on a soporific quality that dumbfounded him. Petty criminals, the dregs of society, taking up his time in a shabby hotel room while he listened to their sordid tales. He had sat, a year earlier, as mediator in a boundary dispute involving some big underworld names in Brooklyn, and it was the peaceful settlement of that potentially dangerous situation which had made his reputation as a gangland mediator. It was a reputation he had never sought and never fully accepted, and yet it stuck and grew through a half-dozen other disputes. He was Arthur Urah, the Arbiter of Uncertainties, the one to call when there was bloodshed to be prevented.

"That's enough for now," he told them finally, pushing back from the card table. "I think I have enough information to reach a decision."

"When?" Rimer asked him.

"Leave me alone for a bit to ponder it all."

They went out of the room, Rimer to the hallway, and Tommy Same to the girl who waited next door. Urah stood and stretched, feeling at that moment every one of his fifty-three years. He walked to the window and looked down at the Sunday afternoon street seven stories below, ominously deserted.

Presently, as he stood there, he heard a footstep on the rug behind him. It was Tommy Same, returned for a few private words. He slipped his arm around Urah's shoulder and spoke in tones of brotherhood. "You and I know how to handle these things, don't we, Arthur? These punks like Rimer have to be coddled just so far. Imagine—sitting down at a table with the guy when I should be kicking his teeth in!"

"Times are changing, Tommy."

"Sure they are. That's why I'm taking over the horse rooms in this town! The day of the independent operator is gone forever."

"Fritz Rimer doesn't think so."

Tommy took his arm away. He was nearly a head shorter than Arthur Urah, and standing there close to him he reminded Urah somehow of the wayward son he'd never had. "Look, Arthur, be good to Rimer. Tell him he's all through and save the poor guy's life."

"You're telling me something, Tommy, and it's not something I want to hear."

"I'm telling you the facts of life in this town. I like to keep everybody happy and look respectable, so I go along with this arbitration bit. But I can't afford to lose the decision. The other thirty-five guys would all bolt if Rimer got away. They wouldn't be still a week."

"So?"

"So you rule against me, Arthur, and I gotta score on Rimer. I'm up against a wall. There's no other way."

"You'd be crazy to try it."

"Arthur . . . I already told Benny. He's waiting out in the hall. If you rule that Rimer stays in business, he never leaves this hotel alive."

Urah stared out the window at the occasional passing cars below. The afternoon shadows were already long, offering a hint of approaching night. "Get out," he said to Tommy. "I'll pretend I never heard that."

"Whatever you say, Arthur."

Then he was gone, and the room was quiet once more. Urah sat down at the card table and began to make a few notes. He'd been at it for ten minutes when another visitor entered through the connecting door.

He glanced up and smiled. "Hello, Sal."

Sally Vogt was a cute blonde trying hard to stay under thirty. Most of the time she succeeded, thanks to her hairdresser. "What have you been doing with yourself lately, Arthur?"

"Bringing people together. Making peace."

"I mean besides that. We used to see you often down at the club."

"That was a long time ago. We travel in different circles now."

"Arthur . . ."

"Yes?"

"He sent me in to talk to you. He thinks he handled it badly."

"He did."

She shifted her feet and gazed at the worn carpet. "He's up tight, Arthur. If he loses control of these horse rooms, he's all finished in the organization. They don't give anybody a second chance."

Arthur Urah shrugged. "Maybe they fire him and hire Fritz Rimer in his place."

"Don't joke, Arthur."

"I'm not. Is he really going to kill Rimer?"

"Of course not!"

"Then what's Benny for? Just to scare people?"

She lit a cigarette and inhaled slowly. "Benny's left over from the old days. Tommy inherited him, along with everything else in town."

"Not quite everything."

"Arthur, Arthur! This isn't your big moment in Brooklyn with the syndicate chiefs. Nobody cares what happens here. Give Tommy Rimer's place and everybody lives in peace."

"You just said Tommy's bosses cared what happened here. That makes it important to him, at least."

"How much would you take to give Tommy the decision, Arthur?"

Urah rubbed a hand across his eyes. "First Tommy, and now you. Do I get Benny in here next, with his gun?"

She didn't answer that. Instead she said, "I suppose you'll make a decision this afternoon."

"There's no reason to delay it. In fact, I think you can tell them to come in now."

As he waited for Rimer and Tommy Same to appear, the room clerk from downstairs stuck his head in the door. "Some of the big boys are waiting in the lobby. They want to know how long you'll be."

"Not long," Urah said, resenting the intrusion. Their presence in the lobby meant that someone didn't trust him to handle the situation.

Fritz Rimer came in alone, shuffling his feet over the faded carpet, hardly able to look at Urah. "It's going bad for me, isn't it?"

"Not so bad."

"Even if I win, I lose. He'll kill me—I know it."

"Then why did you fight him? Why didn't you just pull out?"

"That place is my life. I don't just see my whole life crumple without trying to hang on."

Tommy Same and Sal came in, and she stood behind his chair while they waited for Arthur Urah to deliver his verdict. He cleared his throat and snapped on one of the table lamps, because the room was growing dim in the afternoon twilight.

"I've studied the issues," he began, "and tried to arrive at a fair decision." He cleared his throat once more. Sally Vogt caught his eye and seemed to be telling him something, but he paid no attention. "My ruling is that Fritz Rimer has the right to remain in business as long as he desires. If he should sell his establishment, or pass away, the business should be made part of Tommy's syndicate. But until that time, Rimer is to continue as sole owner and manager."

Tommy leaned back in his chair, saying nothing.

Rimer got to his feet, shaking. "Thanks, Mr. Urah. Thanks for nothing! That decision just sealed my death warrant!"

"You can sell out to Tommy," Arthur pointed out.

"Never! He'll have to kill me if he wants my place!"

"That's something I can arrange," Tommy said quietly.

"There'll be no violence," Urah told them, but even to his own ears the words carried a hollow ring.

Fritz Rimer turned and headed for the door. Tommy Same got up and started after him but then Fritz turned and showed them the little silver pistol in his hand. It looked like a .22, like something he might have borrowed from his wife. "I'm leaving here," he said. "Alive."

Then he was into the hall. Tommy bolted and ran after him, and Arthur was at Tommy's side. Fritz was halfway down the dingy hallway, heading for the elevator, when Benny appeared at the opposite end of the corridor. He saw the gun, and immediately drew his own weapon.

"No!" Sally screamed. "Don't shoot!" but it was too late for anyone to listen now.

Benny fired one quick shot without aiming, and Rimer's little gun coughed in echo. Tommy Same was shouting above the roar, and then he seemed to stumble back into Arthur Urah's arms. He tore free, lurched into the dusty fire hose on the wall, and then fell forward on his face.

"Tommy!" Sally Vogt was on the floor at his side, trying to turn him over, but her left hand came away all bloody from his back and she screamed once more.

Down the hall, Benny had dropped his gun and was running forward. Fritz Rimer simply stared, more terrified than ever, and then he suddenly darted into the elevator. Within moments the room clerk had arrived, summoned by some hotel guest lurking terrified behind his locked door. There were others on the scene, too; the big boys whom Arthur Urah knew so well—Stefenzo and Carlotta and Venice, big men in the syndicate—bigger men than Tommy Same had ever hoped to be.

"What happened?" one of them asked, staring down at the body on the floor. This was Venice, a slim, almost handsome man.

"There was a shooting," Urah explained carefully. "Benny here took a shot at Rimer and missed."

"I didn't mean to," Benny mumbled, too frightened to say more.

The room clerk looked up from the body. "He's dead."

Somebody had taken Sally aside, but her sobbing could still be heard. One of them picked up Benny's fallen gun and brought it down the hall. "This looks too big for the hole in him," somebody observed.

"Search everyone," Stefenzo ordered. "The girl, too."

"Rimer's gone with his gun," Benny said. "He did it, not me."

A quick search of Arthur and Benny and Sal and the dead Tommy revealed no other weapon. There was only Benny's big .38 and the missing gun with which Rimer had fled.

"We don't want the police in on this," Venice told Arthur Urah. "Not yet, anyway. We'll never convince them it was an accident."

"No," Arthur agreed.

They wrapped Tommy Same's body in a sheet and carried it into one of the rooms.

"Check everybody on this floor," Stefenzo ordered the clerk. "Make sure there's no one who'll talk."

"Most of the rooms are empty."

"Check anyway."

Arthur Urah walked past the still stunned Benny and into Sally's room. She was over by the window, staring out at the lights coming on all over the city. "He's dead," she said without emotion to Arthur.

"Yes."

"So what good was all your arbitration? In the end, it came back down to a couple of people shooting it out in a hallway."

"I tried to avoid that."

"Tommy wanted too much. That was always his trouble. Too much. Not thirty-five horse rooms, but thirty-six. He wanted to be too big."

"Yes," Arthur agreed quietly.

She turned suddenly to face him. "What did you do before?" she asked. "Before you started to arbitrate their disputes?"

"Various things. I studied law once."

"But they trust you. Both sides trust you."

"I hope so."

After a time she left him and went in to look at Tommy's body in the next room.

Venice came in to sit with him. "We've taken Benny away," he told Arthur. "He was always a little nuts."

"I suppose so."

"Dangerous."

"Yes."

The telephone rang and Arthur answered it, then passed it to the syndicate man who listened intently. After a moment he held the receiver down against his chest. "They've run Rimer to earth. He's home, packing, apparently getting ready to skip. They want to know if we want him alive or dead."

"Alive," Arthur Urah said without hesitation. "There's been enough killing."

"I suppose so." Then, into the telephone, "Bring him down here."

Arthur Urah sighed and sat down to wait.

An hour later, they had gathered in the room again, around the rickety card table. Rimer was there, under protest, and Benny had been brought back, too. The room clerk from downstairs, and Sally, and the three big men from the syndicate were all seated, their eyes on Urah as he spoke.

"What we have here," he said, "is an interesting problem. We cannot, like the police, dig into Tommy

Same's body and compare bullets under a microscope. We cannot do anything except take testimony and examine the facts. I was there in the hall myself, and I saw what there was to see. The hall, for our purposes, is about fifty feet in length from the door of Tommy's room to the spot where Benny stood. Fritz here was about halfway between the door and Benny, at the elevator, when the shooting started."

"Benny fired toward us," Sally interrupted to explain. "Fritz fired away from us."

"And there was no third shot?" Venice asked in a puzzled tone.

"No."

"Tommy just staggered and fell," Urah said. "And therein would seem to lie the impossibility of the thing. The wound indicates to us a small caliber weapon—as nearly as we can tell without being able to dig for the bullet—yet Rimer's small caliber gun was fired in the opposite direction from where Tommy was standing. Benny's larger gun, fired toward Tommy, would have left a bigger entry hole."

Stefenzo grunted, lifting his bulk from the chair. "Yet there was no other shot, no other gun."

"Why waste time, anyway?" Carlotta asked. "Tommy's death was an accident, no matter how you look at it. The bullet bounced off the wall or something. Let's get on to splitting up his holdings."

"Well, I don't think it was an accident," Sally told them all. "I think he was murdered by Fritz Rimer."

"I didn't . . ." Rimer began, and then fell silent.

Arthur Urah cleared his throat. "I was called in to decide the matter of Rimer's horse room and Tommy Same's claim to it. In that affair, my original judgment of this afternoon still stands. The horse room remains in Rimer's control and, since Tommy is now dead, there's no question of his taking over after Rimer's possible death."

"You can talk about this all you want." Sally told them, "but I'm more interested in how Tommy died." She stormed out into the hall, seeking perhaps some sign, some scrawled revelation on the wall.

"You don't need me for anything," Fritz Rimer said. "Let me get out of here."

"Wait a bit," Carlotta told him.

"I have a business to attend to!"

"On Sunday night? Wait a bit."

Arthur Urah interrupted. "Let him go. The killing of Tommy was accidental."

Rimer left, a little man and fearful. Then they settled down to the business at hand. In the hour that followed, Tommy Same's empire was divided. Arthur Urah listened to it all, taking little part in the discussions. This was not his job, and he would only be needed if a dispute arose. He wandered over to the window at one point, and then into the next room. It was there that Sally Vogt found him.

"I was in the hall," she said.

"Yes?"

"If you look, you can see the marks where both bullets hit the wall."

"I didn't look." He was starting to zip his briefcase. It was time to be going home.

"Arthur . . ." Sally hesitated.

"What is it, Sally?"

"Are they still in the next room?"

"Yes. The territory has to be reassigned."

"Reassigned. Tommy dies, and the territory is reassigned."

"Life must go on, Sal. You know that."

"And what about his body, wrapped in a sheet like some mummy?"

"The body will be given a decent burial."

"In the Jersey dumps?"

"Sal . . ."

"The wound was in his back, Arthur. In his *back!* He was facing the other two, but you were right behind him. He stumbled into you, just before he fell."

"I had no gun," Arthur Urah said quietly.

"No, but you had this!" She brought her hand into view and dropped the ice pick on the low table between them. "Tommy wasn't shot by a small caliber bullet at all! He was stabbed with this ice pick just as the other two fired at each other. Then, while we bent over the body, you simply pushed the ice pick up the nozzle of the fire hose in the hall—where I just found it."

"You try too hard, Sally. You look too closely. This world isn't made for people who look too closely, who find ice picks in fire hoses."

"You killed him because he wouldn't go along with your settlement, because he was going to get Rimer."

"Perhaps I killed him to save Rimer's life, Sally."

"I'm going in there and tell them, Arthur," she said. "It won't bring Tommy back, but at least it'll avenge him just a little."

She had moved toward the door when he reached out to stop her. "Not that way, Sally. Listen a bit."

"To what? To the Arbiter of Uncertainties, while he foxes out another decision? What will it be this time, Arthur? What will they give you when I walk in there and tell them? Life or death?"

"You don't understand, Sal."

"I understand! I'm going to tell them."

"You don't have to. They know."

She paused again, backing against the coffee table, staring at him with widening eyes. "They know?"

"You asked once what I did before I became the Arbiter. I did many things, Sally. Some of them with an ice pick," he admitted.

"No!"

"Tommy was getting too big. They wanted his territory. They thought Fritz might do the job for them, but Fritz was a coward. When I saw my opportunity, there in the hall, I had to take it."

"And all this talk, this investigation?"

"For your benefit, Sally. And Benny's."

"If they won't do it, Arthur, I will." She bent down for the ice pick again, but he merely brushed it away, onto the floor.

"Get out, Sally. You don't want to get hurt."

"Damn you! You're not even human, Arthur! You're some sort of monster!"

He smiled sadly. He'd been called worse things in

his life. He picked up the ice pick and dropped it into the briefcase, and finished zipping it shut.

After a time, when Sally had gone, he went down in the elevator. He nodded to the room clerk as he passed, and then went out into the night.

SLOW MOTION MURDER

(Novelette)

Richard Hardwick

The reason for old Gus Johnson's almost unintelligible call was sitting with his back against the wall inside the boathouse. It was Bernie Hibler, or more correctly, it was the mortal coil which Bernie had shuffled off rather recently and abruptly. He had been hog-tied to a stout wall beam, blindfolded, gagged, and shot squarely in the chest.

"I ain't touched a thing since I found him," Gus vowed to Sheriff Dan Peavy. Gus operated a little bait place on the creek about a quarter of a mile back, at the junction of the main road. "Well, nothin' except when I went in the house to phone you and Deputy Miller."

Dan Peavy nodded, then knelt and touched the body. "Still warm, Pete," he said, glancing up at me. "Ain't been dead too long." His gaze shifted to Gus. "How'd you happen to find him?"

The old fellow didn't seem entirely steady on his feet. One reason was probably the shock of finding the dead man. Another reason could be detected easily anywhere downwind of him. He was pretty well smashed. "Well, Dan, you know we been havin' this dang northeaster for the better part of a week now, and any fool knows the fishin' ain't any good while a northeaster's blowin'. No reason for anybody to wanta buy bait, so when the weather's like this I allus use the time to kinda catch up on my rest."

"Been catchin' up on your drinkin' too, ain't you, Gus?"

The old man bent his head and nodded seriously. "A mite, I reckon. Not too much, mind you. Everything in moderation. Anyhow, all day I been sort of nappin' off

and on. Along about three or four o'clock this afternoon I woke up and had me a little nip, and just as I
was layin' back down on my cot I heard somethin'
from down this way toward Hibler's. Sounded like a
shotgun goin' off. I figured it was just Bernie blastin' a
varmint, and I went on back to sleep."

"You say that was about three or four o'clock?" I
asked him. "How do you know?"

"I'm kinda guessin' at that. You see, I had me another little nip at two. I noticed the clock then. And
later on, when that dang car woke me up, it was right
at four-thirty. So it musta been around three or four
when I got up in between."

"What car?" asked Dan.

"Her car! She was tearin' outta Hibler's road like the
devil was after her. Didn't even stop when she hit the
main road; just laid it over on two wheels, and
hightailed on towards town. All that racket woulda
woke up a dead man!"

"You said her? Who're you talkin' about?"

"I thought I told you! It was Mollie Hammond."

I stared at the old man. "Mollie *Ham*mond?" I
couldn't believe it.

Mollie was one of the finest young women in Guale
County, and lately, one of the unluckiest. Barely
twenty-five, she was already a widow. Sam Hammond
missed a turn a couple of months before on the old
post road. The big live oak he tangled with survived.
Sam didn't.

It wasn't more than a day after the funeral that Mollie learned Sam had put every dime they had into some
kind of deal with Bernie Hibler. Bernie insisted the
deal had fizzled, and that his and Sam's money had
gone down the drain.

"Afraid it was Mollie, right enough," Gus said.
"That got me to wonderin'. From everything I been
hearin', I'd say Mollie was about the last person in
Guale County to pay a friendly visit to Hibler. I ain't
got a phone, so I got in my pickup and drove down
here to his place." He nodded toward the body.
"That's what I found."

"Whatd'ya think, Pete?" Dan Peavy asked.

I shrugged. "Same as you do, I suppose. There was plenty of folks said Hibler out and out swindled her. I guess Mollie could have done it, but I'd sure like to hear what she's got to say."

Dan turned to Gus. "You didn't see her drive in here, huh?"

"Nope. She musta come in a lot quieter than she come out. And like I said——"

"I know," Dan nodded tiredly. "You were nippin' and nappin'."

Bernie Hibler wasn't exactly a hermit, but he did treasure his privacy. His place was on a point overlooking Frenchman's Creek in the northwest corner of Guale County, about twenty miles out from the county seat. The boathouse was on a small tidewater, maybe a hundred feet back from Frenchman's Creek, and the same distance from the house proper. There was a permanent deck inside that ran the length of the little building. A ladder led down to a floating dock in the boat slip, the usual arrangement to accommodate the six-foot rise and fall of the tide along our part of the coast.

The boat slip was empty, which prompted Dan to ask Gus if he knew where the boat might be.

"Hibler was havin' some work done on it down at the county marina while the weather was so poor."

Dan walked down the deck, looking around. It was pretty much the same as any other boathouse; coils of rope hung from pegs on the wall, there were a couple of cast nets, a lantern, and half a dozen fishing rods of assorted sizes were hanging from nails. A tackle box and a large bait bucket sat side by side at the edge of the deck just above the float, and a rigged fishing rod lay nearby. The line was tangled around the end of the rod, as if it had been dropped or thrown down hurriedly. A couple of yards of line dangled over the edge where the hook, which still had a piece of shrimp on it, had snagged on the planking of the floating dock.

Bernie Hibler had been a particular sort of fisherman, despite his other drawbacks, and it would have been a cool day you-know-where before he was that careless and messy with his equipment.

"You best have a look in the house, too," Gus said. "The whole place was a real mess when I went in there to phone you boys." The old fisherman scratched his head uncertainly. "Do you reckon I finished doin' my duty, Dan? I'd sure like to get on back to my cabin."

Dan Peavy nodded absently, his puzzled attention being on the dead man. "Yeah, Gus, you run on. Don't stray far, though, in case we need you."

As Gus hobbled out to his pickup truck Dan said to me, "I can't figure this business about tyin' him up, blindfoldin' him, and puttin' that dang gag in his mouth." He gave a gentle twist to the lumpy end of his nose. "You called Doc before we left town, didn't you?"

"Right." I could see the dirt road through the open door. "Fact is, here he comes now."

"Good. Call in and tell Jerry to pick up Mollie Hammond. Tell him to bring her out here."

Guale County's beloved physician and coroner pulled up in the ambulance from the funeral parlor. "County's gettin' to be worse than New York City," he grumbled as he put his black satchel down alongside the body of Bernie Hibler. "Murders, gangsters . . ."

"How soon can you give me some idea on the time of death?" Dan asked him.

"What's your hurry?"

"We got a suspect, and the time might be right important."

"I'll narrow it down after the autopsy, but I'll see what I can do to oblige you now."

I used the interval to radio the office and get Deputy Jerry Sealey started on his task, and then I met Dan inside Hibler's house. Gus Johnson had been right; the place was a real mess. Drawers were pulled out and stuff thrown all about, furniture overturned, cabinets open with all the contents on the floor. Whoever had done it either had been looking for something, or wanted to make us think he had.

"There's always been tales around that Hibler kept a

lot of cash out here, Dan," I said. "Maybe that's what happened."

"Maybe. Still can't figure what he's doin' out there in the boathouse, though. Looks to me like if somebody was goin' to shoot him, he'd have just *shot* him."

"And speaking of shooting," I said, "I haven't seen a gun anywhere around here. Hibler must have had a shotgun."

"He had one," Dan said. "I've seen it. A double-barrel twelve gauge. And you're right, it ain't here."

"Reckon the killer must have taken it when he left."

He looked around at me. "Or *she?*"

We returned to the dock where Doc Stebbins was just closing up his little bag. "Well, it's five after six now. Judgin' from the body temperature, state o' rigor mortis, blood coagulation, he was probably alive at two o'clock, Dan. And he was probably dead by, oh, maybe four. That much spread help you any?"

Dan Peavy sighed. "Helps me, Doc. But I'm afraid it ain't gonna help Mollie Hammond much."

The old medic's eyebrows lifted. "Mollie? What's she got to do with this?"

"That's our suspect," I said, and went on to tell him what Gus had said.

"I'd stake every dime I got on that girl!" Doc exploded. "Why, that girl couldn'ta done this!"

"What makes you say so?"

"Well, she . . . she just *couldn'ta!*"

"Right now it's just her word against Gus', of course," I said hopefully. "That is, if she denies being out here."

"What about Gus himself?" Doc suggested. He snapped his fingers. "I'll tell you right now who to start lookin' for. Fred Trent! That no-good bum has threatened Hibler plenty of times; in front of witnesses, too! He coulda tied him up and shot him, and enjoyed every minute of it!"

Dan shook his head. "He's the first one I thought about when I heard somebody had murdered Hibler."

"Right!" said Doc. "He's always hated Bernie Hibler, and that judgment Bernie got against him a few months back just might have been the last straw."

The judgment Doc had reference to was five hundred dollars the court had awarded Hibler after Fred Trent, three sheets to the wind, had smacked into Bernie's car in the middle of town and ripped off a fender and a few other things.

"There's only one thing wrong with figuring Trent did this," Dan said. "He's got an ironclad alibi."

"Ironclad my foot! Ain't no such thing!"

"Afraid this time there is." Dan Peavy sighed and scratched his head through his bushy white hair. *"I'm* his alibi. Trent's been workin' for the county all week, and since eight o'clock this morning he's been paintin' the inside of the jail."

By the time Deputy Jerry Sealey arrived with Mollie Hammond, Doc had wound up everything he could do on the scene, and Hibler's body had been taken back to town for the autopsy. Bloodstains and a chalk outline were all that remained to indicate what had happened.

"I didn't know what to tell her, Dan," Jerry said. "I just said you wanted to see her."

"What's this all about, Sheriff Peavy?" Mollie wanted to know. She was a pretty little thing in a tired sort of way, with big brown eyes and a worried look. You couldn't help but wonder what a new hair-do and some makeup would do for her.

"You were out here this afternoon, weren't you, Mollie?" Dan asked.

She frowned. "Why do you ask?"

"We got somebody says he saw you leavin' here in your car about four-thirty. Gus Johnson. He's got a shack up at the junction o' the main road—"

She drew herself up, as if preparing for an ordeal. "I won't deny it, Sheriff. I was here."

"Something's happened out here, Mollie," I said. "Something bad."

She nodded, not looking directly at me. "I—I know. Bernie Hibler's been shot. He's dead."

"I reckon you know your legal rights," Dan said. "Maybe you best get a lawyer."

"I didn't do it! That was why I was driving so fast by Gus Johnson's place. I was scared! I found his body out in the boathouse when I got here, and I never saw anything like that before in my life! I—I was scared half to death!"

"Kind of unusual you bein' out here, wouldn't you say?" Dan asked her.

"I wouldn't have been here at all if Hibler hadn't phoned me and asked me to come. He called me at about four o'clock. He said he'd decided to settle up with me, and for me to come out here before he changed his mind. At first I thought it was some kind of a joke, that maybe it wasn't Hibler at all. So, when he hung up, I tried to phone him back. He wouldn't answer, and there wasn't anything for me to do but come out and see what it was all about. Well, I knocked on the door, and when nobody came I walked out here to the boathouse, and I found him, tied up and all that blood."

"He called you at four?" I said.

She nodded. "I remember looking at the clock. It's only about five miles over here from my house, and I left after I tried to call him back. I don't suppose I was here more than five minutes or so before I discovered this terrible . . ."

"Was anybody with you when you got this call?"

"No. Since—since Sam was killed things have been pretty tough for me, and I've been taking in sewing. I was working when he called."

Dan scratched his chin. "I don't reckon I have to tell you how this is gonna look to some folks, Mollie."

"They'll think I killed Hibler? But I didn't, Sheriff Peavy! I swear I didn't! He was dead when I got here!"

"How come you didn't call us, Mollie?" Jerry said. "If you'd of called us, then it woulda looked a lot better."

"I was plain scared. I—I knew how it would look, and I guess I figured if nobody knew I was out here I would be better off." She looked at Dan Peavy. "Are—are you going to arrest me?"

"No. Jerry'll take you home, Mollie. But I'm gonna have to ask you to stay there till you hear from me."

Doc Stebbins got a preliminary autopsy report to the

sheriff's office at eleven that night. It backed up what he had said before, about the time of death being between two and four in the afternoon.

"Couldn't narrow it down any closer than that," the coroner said. "That close enough to do any good?"

"Reckon it'll have to be."

"There were a couple other things might interest you. There was a bruise on his head; looked like a hard enough blow to knock him out."

"Which could explain how the killer managed to get him all tied up that way," Jerry suggested.

"And," Doc went on, "the angle of the wound was right interesting. The way it looked to me, he was shot right where the body was found, sittin' propped against the wall. If that was the case, the killer musta been lying down on the deck when he shot him. The gun, by my figurin', couldn'ta been more'n six or eight inches off the floor."

"There could be another explanation for that," I put in. There was a tide table in the desk drawer and I pulled it out and ran my finger down the low tide column. "Yeah, look here. The tide was low this afternoon at 4:42. Now if Hibler was shot at, say, four o'clock, the tide would have been pretty nearly out. A man standing on the floating dock, maybe just about to get into a boat and leave, would have been able to lay the gun right over the edge of the deck and let loose!"

"It makes sense," admitted Jerry.

Dan Peavy nodded skeptically. "There's a lot of screwy angles to this thing. Pete, you and Jerry check up and down Frenchman's Creek first thing in the morning. Maybe you can find somebody that saw something."

"Like what?" asked Jerry.

"Like a boat," Dan snapped. " 'Specially like a boat somewhere near Hibler's place."

Just then there was the sound of tires squealing up to the curb outside. A door slammed and old Gus Johnson came wheezing into the office.

"Just remembered something, Dan! Dang if I know

how come I was to overlook it before! There *was* another car come outta Hibler's road today! It was that old rattle trap o' Fred Trent's!"

"I was right!" boomed Doc Stebbins, slamming his hand down on the desk. "I told you so, didn't I!"

Dan Peavy held up one hand for silence. "What time was this, Gus?"

"Time? Oh, it was about seven-thirty this mornin'. Dunno what time he drove into Hibler's. I woke up 'bout quarter past and was havin' a bite o' breakfast when I seen him drive out."

Dan looked over at Doc. "Hibler couldn'ta been dead that long, could he?"

The coroner's jaw knotted and he shook his head. "No, he couldn'ta!"

The northeaster was over. At daybreak next morning the sky was clean and blue, with just a zephyr of a breeze from the south. Jerry and I launched the county's boat at the Frenchman's Landing ramp and headed upstream, stopping at every house, shack, fishing camp, everywhere, in fact, that we could find somebody to talk to. We found one other boat on the creek, a crab fisherman tending his traps. The answer was the same everywhere. The only boat anybody had seen on the river all day was the crab boat.

Jerry and I both knew him, a fellow by the name of Lewis, from up Cypress City way.

"Who is it you're looking for?" he asked us.

"Ain't exactly sure," Jerry said. "The guy what murdered Bernie Hibler, whoever it is."

Lewis' eyes popped. "That's the first I heard of any murder. When did it happen?"

"You'll read about it in the paper. We got to get moving," I said.

On the way back to town Jerry said, "What about him, Pete? What about Lewis? He was out there on Frenchman's Creek yesterday. All he woulda had to do was run his boat into Hibler's place and nobody woulda been the wiser. That business just now coulda been an act."

"And what about any of the others we talked to?

Seems to me with traffic as light as it was on the water yesterday, pretty near anybody with a boat could have sneaked over there without being seen."

"Yeah," he mumbled, slouching down in the car seat, "I see whatcha mean."

I knew what was on Jerry's mind, the same thing that was bothering me more with each dead end we hit. The fear that we were going to wind up with Mollie Hammond when everything else had fizzled out.

We had started early, and it was just after nine-thirty when we arrived at the office. Fred Trent's car pulled up right in back of us.

"You boys just gettin' to work, too?" he said somewhat pointedly.

"We been working, Trent," Jerry said. "Which seems to be more'n you been doin'."

"Didn't feel so hot this morning," he said. "Pretty near didn't make it atall."

Dan Peavy met us at the door. "Want a word with you, Trent," he said.

"You fellas caught Bernie's murderer yet?" Trent said.

"You heard about it, huh?"

Trent walked to the desk, nodding. "Yeah. Stopped on the way in this morning to get me a cup o' coffee. Everybody was talkin' about it. Just goes to show, you never know."

"What does that mean?" I asked him.

He looked around at me. "Just that you never know when you see somebody but what it'll be the last time. I seen Bernie myself yesterday morning. Stopped by his place about seven on my way to work. That dang judgment he got against me, I been payin' him twenty-five a month on it." He fumbled in his shirt pocket and dropped a piece of paper on the desk. "There's the receipt he give me. Musta been about the last thing he signed his name to."

Dan Peavy glanced at the paper. We hadn't found any money, either in the house or on the body. Unless Hibler had gone out during the day—and we had no reason to assume he had—there should have been at least twenty-five dollars somewhere out there. It looked now like robbery had been part of it.

"What was it you wanted to talk to me about, Sheriff Peavy?" Trent said.

Dan gave the end of his nose a little tug. "I reckon you just about covered it, Trent. Now then, how about gettin' busy and finish up this paint job?"

Dan checked with the bank and found out that Hibler carried a checking account with them.

"There's always been talk around that he kept a good bit o' money out there at his house," Dan said. "You set any store in this?"

The banker nodded. "I'm right sure he did. Bernie was always working on some kind of deal and he liked to have cash to work with."

"You have any idea how much he mighta kept, or where he kept it?"

"As for where, your guess is good as mine. As for how much, well, that'd be a plain guess, too. I'd say he had at least two thousand dollars cash all the time. Maybe more, but two thousand would be the absolute minimum."

I was thinking about Mollie Hammond, taking in sewing to make a living. Two thousand would be a lot of money to her; two thousand, along with some revenge.

And what about Gus Johnson? Or the crab fisherman?

"How's the case going?" the banker asked Dan.

"As good as we could expect," Dan answered guardedly.

"There's talk around town that the thing's cut and dried. Folks say Mollie Hammond admitted being out there about the time Hibler was shot."

"Like I say, it's goin' about as good as we could hope for."

"It don't look too good for Mollie, does it?" I said to Dan on the way back to the office.

"Not with folks around town startin' to talk against her, it don't. Pete, how come half the folks in this county ain't got sense enough to come in outta the rain, and yet they can all figure out a murder case in five minutes?"

He wasn't really expecting an answer, and of course, he didn't get one.

Doc was at the office when we got there, along with Jerry. The coroner was sitting at Dan's desk.

"There's something else about Hibler's body," he said. "The time of death is the same as I said it was, but the marks where his arms were tied look to me like he might have been tied up for a considerable time before he was shot."

Dan filled a cup at the water cooler. "Got any idea how long?"

" 'Fraid not. Might have been less than an hour, actually, dependin' on how hard he tried to get loose."

"You know," Dan said, coming over and slouching down on the corner of the desk, "that's the part o' this thing that I just can't figure. If you was gonna shoot a man, how come you'd go to all the trouble o' tying him up that way, and what the devil was the idea of the blindfold and the gag? It just don't make any sense at all!"

"It makes plenty of sense to me," Jerry said. "Fact is, I'm kinda surprised none of you figured it out."

"Is that so?" Dan said. "Then how about tellin' us?"

"It's a smoke screen, pure and simple. Same with that business of the fishing rod and the bait bucket and the tackle box. The killer did every bit o' that just to get us to puzzling over it."

"Could be he's right," I said. Up to now, it was the only thing that made any sense.

"Alright," said Dan. "Then gettin' back to what you might say is our number one suspect, Mollie Hammond, how come she'd have the time and patience to do all that and then go flyin' outta there right past old Gus Johnson's shack, makin' enough racket to wake him up, and even admit she was there when we told her she had been seen?"

"That's simple, too," Jerry said. "She ain't the murderer."

But at that point, even Doc Stebbins looked a bit skeptical about it.

I knew it the second Jerry walked into the cafe. There was that telltale gleam in his eye as he took the vacant stool next to mine. "Pete—"

It was late afternoon and I had plans for that night. I lifted both hands. "Don't say it! You've got an idea?"

Jerry nodded, his prominent Adam's apple bobbing an accompaniment. "Not just an idea, but a *great* idea. Listen, unless it was somebody we ain't even got a lead on, it stands to reason that from the point of motive it coulda been either Mollie or Fred Trent, right?"

"Right, but—"

"But Trent's got an alibi, so that narrows it down to Mollie. Alright. Then, from the point o' view of opportunity, it coulda been Mollie or Gus Johnson, right? And if robbery was the motive, it still coulda been Gus. Right?"

"Sure, but—"

"Now me and you both know a sweet girl like Mollie Hammond couldn't have done what was done out there to Hibler, right?"

"I suppose you might say that."

"So, where does that leave us?" he asked, grinning slyly.

I stared at him for several seconds, letting all that deduction sift through the gray matter again. It still came out a little confused. "I see what you're getting at. You're saying Gus did it, and you're saying that by the process of elimination. But let me remind you of something, Deputy Sealey; in the good old United States, a man's innocent till proven guilty. And you haven't proved a thing!"

"Ah ha! You're absolutely correct! But in my book, every criminal has a weak spot. All you have to do is find that weak spot, zero in on it with all you've got, and the next thing you know he's behind bars! And that's where my idea comes in."

I got up and tossed a dime to Thelma for my coffee. "Well, you and your idea sit right here and talk to each other. I've been in on some of your schemes, if you'll recall. I'm not having any tonight, Deputy. Fact is, I'm taking Juanita to the drive-in movie, and that's that."

I knew it when I said it. I couldn't get that skinny screwball off my mind.

I sat there staring blankly at the silver screen, Juanita's head on my shoulder, and all I could think about was Jerry.

"What do you suppose he's doing?"

"What'd you say, Pete?" Juanita murmured, digging into the popcorn box.

"Huh? Oh, I guess I was just thinking out loud."

Juanita snuggled up a little closer and just then a head poked in the window on my side of the car. It was the theatre manager. "Deputy Miller, there's a message for you to call the Bon Air Cafe. You can use the phone over at the refreshment stand."

Juanita pulled away. "Is that Thelma calling you?"

"It might be important. I'll be right back."

I made the call and Thelma told me that Jerry had left an envelope there for me. "He knew you'd be at the movie," she said, "and he made me promise to call you at ten-thirty. I . . . I really didn't want to, Pete." It was kind of touchy, because I dated Thelma quite a bit, too. I was on the spot.

"Alright," I said. "Open the envelope and read it to me."

"Jerry said nobody was to open it but you."

My blood pressure started rising. As soon as the movie was over Juanita and I had planned to drive out to the beach. The moon was full and there's nothing like a walk on the beach in the moonlight to . . .

"Pete," Thelma said. "There's a customer coming in. I gotta go. You'd better come see about this note. It might be real important."

Juanita wasn't any happier about it than I was as I pulled up in front of the Bon Air Cafe. I trotted inside and Thelma handed me the envelope, pausing long enough to throw a disapproving glance toward the car, where Juanita was pointedly applying lipstick.

Jerry's note was as short as it was cryptic. It read:

I'm putting the pressure on Gus Johnson's weak

spot. Get out to his place as soon as you read this and, if everything works out as planned, you just might get to see a real lawman in action.

JS

That did it. I crumpled the note and jammed it into my pocket. As I strode out to the car I noticed the lights were on in the sheriff's office across the street, and I could see the top of Dan Peavy's head there at his desk. I knew this case had him going, and there might be a chance that Jerry was onto something. I had no choice but to follow through on it.

"Nothing's wrong, is it, Pete?" Juanita asked.

I gripped the windowsill with both hands. "It's like this—"

"We're not going out to the beach?" The dreamy expression she had featured all evening was no longer in evidence. In its place was something more tight-lipped.

"It's the Hibler case."

The door flew open, almost knocking me down. "Alright, *Mis*ter Miller! Al*right!*" She walked rapidly away down the sidewalk, glancing over her shoulder only long enough to say, "Call me sometime, when you're not so *busy!*"

"Juanita! Let me explain! *Juanita!*"

"The great lover having trouble?" somebody said behind me. I didn't even have to look to know it was Thelma.

I went across the street to the office, fighting a number of conflicting urges, many of which were not at all in keeping with my oath as a deputy, to uphold the law.

I uncrumpled Jerry's note and dropped it on Dan Peavy's desk.

"I have no idea what it means," I said. "All I know is, he messed up a right promising evening, and whatever this is all about, it better be good!"

It was nearly midnight when Dan and I got out to Gus Johnson's bait shack. The moon was high, and the creek and the marshes beyond the cabin were almost as bright as day.

Jerry's car stood beside Gus' pickup truck, and lights were on inside the shack. As soon as we stopped the car and shut off the engine, we heard the singing. It was coming from the shack, two voices loudly but unsuccessfully trying to harmonize on *Bluetail Fly*. The place was a musical disaster area.

"What in the name o'—" Dan growled.

I was beginning to suspect something, but there was little point in venturing a guess in view of the fact we would know in a matter of seconds. The door was open and we stepped inside. There were Gus and Jerry, sitting at a rickety old table, heads thrown back, caterwauling like a pair of hoarse beagles baying at the moon. On the table were two glasses and a quart bottle of Old Sourmash. Jerry had indeed lashed out at Gus' weakness.

Deputy Sealey spotted us and lurched to his feet, grinning like an idiot. "Look who's here!" He shook Gus, who was still singing. "We got comp'ny! Where's your manners? Get 'em a glass!"

"Never mind the glass," said Dan. "I think you just better come on home with us, Deputy."

Jerry came around the table, one finger to his lips in an obvious effort to shut Dan up. When he was closer he whispered, "I done it! I got him t' confess! Now you all just sit tight and I'll get him to do it again!"

"Confess?"

Jerry's head rocked up and down. "Just come right out and asked him if he didn't shoot him, and he said he sure did, and was proud of it! Listen . . ." He faced around and headed back to the table like he was battling a high wind. He picked up the bottle of Old Sourmash and poured the last of it into Gus' glass. "Drink up, ol' pal. Drink up, and tell me once more how you wanted to do it for a long time, and you fin'ly got your scattergun and let him have it. C'mon and tell ol' Jer."

Gus guzzled down the booze and stood up. "Better'n that, ol' pal, I'm gonna *show* ya! Jush a secon' . . ." He staggered through a door and reappeared carrying a long double barrelled shotgun. "Lesh go outside. C'mon, everybody. Everybody c'mon with me."

"Dan," I whispered. "Dan, maybe we better take that thing away from him before somebody gets hurt—or killed."

"In a minute," Dan said. "Let's see what he's got in mind. We just mighta underestimated Jerry."

Gus made it through the front door on the second try and with Jerry, Dan, and myself bringing up the rear, he headed out the narrow dock over the creek. At the end of the dock he stopped. Jerry draped one arm around the old man's shoulders, winked broadly at Dan and me, and said, "Now, ol' buddy, show us how you gunned him down!"

Gus nodded, lifted the big gun unsteadily to his shoulder, pointed it out over the marsh, and pulled both triggers.

It sounded like a baby atom bomb going off. But even as the blast faded away, the tremendous recoil of the two shells sent both Gus and Jerry flying backward where they vanished in the creek amid a great splash.

Jerry was the first to surface, coughing and spluttering and yelling, *"You heard him! What'd I tell ya!"*

Gus bobbed up and I managed to grab his arm before he went down again. Dan had hold of Jerry and we dragged them both up onto the dock, wet and soggy.

"Put the cuffs on him, Dan!" Jerry squealed. "You heard him! That's how he shot Bernie Hibler!"

Gus wavered back and forth, tilting his head to drain the water out of his right ear. "Bernie?" he said. He started to laugh and then he draped his arm around Jerry. "Wuz it Bernie you wuz talkin' about, ol' pal? Why dincha shay so? I didn't shoot ol' *Bernie!* I wuz talkin' about that buck I shot back in '53. Bigges' deer ever come outta Guale County!" He started back toward the shack with Jerry. "Shay, ol' pal, reckon you got any more o' that stuff in your car?"

Dan gave Jerry the morning off next day. Even so, when he reported in at two p.m., he was not a well man. His hangover was surpassed only by his desire for silence on the happenings of the previous night. But there are some people who do not go along with the theory of letting sleeping dogs lie. I'm one of them.

"You ever seen a real lawman in action, Jerry?" I asked.

He was at the water cooler, for the fifteenth time. "Pete, how's about knocking it off? I *still* think he done it. It's just that, well, the old codger's a lot smarter'n I give him credit for being. I'll figure something out yet!"

Dan Peavy came in, and right away I could tell something had happened. He wasn't exactly smiling, but there was a look of possible discovery on his weathered face.

"Deputy Sealey, it come to me while I was havin' lunch!" he said, clapping his junior deputy on the shoulder. "It might be you cracked this murder case without even knowin' it! Come on, let's me and you take a little ride and see if I'm right!"

"You mean you think Gus done it? How . . ."

"Never mind the questions right now. Pete, you stick here at the office and be sure Fred Trent gets that paintin' done. I might need you to round up the suspects if this pans out."

I'd worked for Dan Peavy long enough to know he had said his last word on the subject, so I did as I was told.

After Dan and Jerry drove away, I busied myself catching up on a little paper work, and when that was done I phoned Juanita down at the bus station and tried to soft soap her about last night. It took about ten minutes of talk, but I managed to get a date with her for the following Friday night.

Dan called in at about four o'clock, and I could tell by the tone of his voice he was onto something; he'd found a lead.

"Pete, I want you to get Trent and Mollie, and have the lot of 'em out here at Hibler's boathouse at five o'clock sharp. You got that? Five sharp, without fail!"

"How come—"

"Don't ask fool questions! Just be here!"

Fred Trent was no problem. He was right there, still painting the inside of the jail.

I phoned Mollie's house and told her I'd pick her up in half an hour.

"What for, Pete?" she asked.

I could almost see those big brown eyes, scared, wondering what was going to happen to her. I wanted to say something encouraging, but I couldn't. "Now you try not to worry, Mollie. Dan Peavy's got some kind of idea about this, and he wants everybody out there."

When I told Fred to put away his paint and brushes and come with me, he put up a bit of a squawk. "What for, Miller? I got work to do here! I ain't got time to go traipsin' all over the county, like some folks I know."

"Look, Trent," I said, beginning to wear a little thin myself. "All I know is we're investigating a murder. Now when the sheriff tells me to bring some folks to where he is, I'm going to bring 'em. One way or another, so move."

He muttered something, and began to clean his brush. Frankly, I was puzzled about Dan wanting him out there. There didn't seem to be any way he could figure in it, unless he had an accomplice.

Trent and I went by Mollie's house and picked her up, and the three of us drove out to Hibler's. It was a quiet drive. Mollie seemed too scared to carry on any conversation, and Fred seemed too mad. I would have been glad to talk to either one of them, but it just didn't work out that way.

We were five minutes ahead of the prescribed time, and Dan Peavy met us outside the boathouse as we all got out of the car.

Gus Johnson was sitting in Dan's car.

The sheriff took off his hat. "Mollie. Trent. Glad Pete was able to get you both out here. I think we just might be about to wind this whole thing up."

"Yeah?" said Trent. "Well, unless all of us done it, how come you just didn't get the guilty one out here?"

"Because we ain't . . ." Dan grinned and waved over toward the boathouse. "Like somebody said, one picture's worth a mess o' words. Let's all step inside and see if I can conjure up a picture o' what happened."

Jerry was standing inside on the upper deck, smiling like he knew something, or thought he did. Everything seemed to be about the same as it had been, with the exception that the body was gone, and just the chalk marks and the bloodstain to show where it had been.

Then I saw something else was different. There was a double barrelled shotgun lying on the heavy beam at the edge of the dock. It was upside down, the stock sticking out over the edge, and the barrel pointed squarely at the outline where Hibler's body had been. The barrel was wedged in between the tackle box and the bait bucket.

Dan Peavy turned around to the little group, like a sightseeing guide. His cold gray eyes stopped on Trent. "That's Hibler's gun, the one that was missin' from the house."

"Where the devil did you find it?" Gus Johnson asked.

"We'll get around to that in a minute," said Dan. "First things first. Now, if it was Mollie who shot him—"

"I *swear* I didn't do it, Sheriff Peavy!" she broke in.

"I said *if*. If it was Mollie, she coulda got rid o' the gun in a thousand places after she left here. And if it was Gus, he coulda done the same thing. Neither one o' them had an alibi for hardly any part of the afternoon. But we found the gun not more'n twenty feet from where the body was, so . . ."

"I don't understand," Gus said. "I seen you fellas look all around here, and you didn't find no gun."

"We didn't look in the water," said Dan. "That's where the gun was."

He looked over at Jerry. "About time, ain't it, Deputy?"

"Right."

Dan nodded. "Rig it up."

Jerry went around the shotgun, picked up the tip of the fishing rod that had been lying there when the body was found, and slipped the tip inside the trigger guard of the shotgun. Then he stepped back. "Any second now."

The line still hung down to the float below, but now the tide was almost at ebb, and instead of being slack like it was the day of the murder, it was almost taut.

"Now then, everybody watch," said Dan Peavy.

"Any second—" Jerry started to say again.

But he was interrupted by three things in rapid succession. First, there was a mighty blast as the fishing rod pulled the trigger of the gun. Second, the recoil sent the gun sailing out to splash into the boat slip and disappear. And third, Fred Trent let out a yell and made a lunge for the door.

He was halfway to the main road before Jerry and I caught up to him in the patrol car.

Fred Trent confessed that he had killed Hibler for revenge and money. After he had paid Hibler the twenty-five dollars the morning of the day of the murder, Trent drove away from the house. But he stopped beyond a clump of bushes, sneaked back, and peeped through a window. He saw Hibler stashing the money away, waited till Bernie came outside, and conked him on the head. He had figured out what he was going to do, and he carried the unconscious man to the boathouse, tied him to the beam. The blindfold was so Hibler wouldn't see what was in store for him, and maybe twist loose or at least get out of the line of fire. The gag was just in case somebody came around during the day.

Trent had figured the tide carefully. At seven that morning the tide was coming in. He rigged up the murder apparatus, reeling off just enough line so that it would tighten an hour before low tide in the afternoon. When everything was set, he took Hibler's money, messed the house up to try to throw a wrench into the investigation, then drove on into town to set up an alibi that nobody could question.

At four that afternoon he had gone across the street to the Bon Air for a cup of coffee. He had phoned Mollie from there, acting like he was Hibler and telling her to come out to talk about Sam Hammond's money. Mollie, as he knew, would give us a first-class suspect. About the time he was talking to Mollie, the shotgun discharged out at Hibler's.

Well, we had Trent behind bars where he belonged, and Dan Peavy answered a few questions.

"What put you onto Trent?" I asked him. "Especially, since you were his alibi?"

"First off," he said, giving Mollie a paternal smile, "I couldn't bring myself to believe Mollie could do a thing like that. Then there was all that fishin' tackle layin' around the boathouse, and I knew Hibler was too good a fisherman to waste his time in a northeaster. 'Course, there was Fred Trent himself, working like a dog all day, with just a couple of short coffee breaks. He never was outta sight the whole day, and that just wasn't like Fred Trent." He grinned and looked over at Jerry. "And there was Deputy Sealey's night out at Gus Johnson's place when that gun kicked 'em both into the creek. It hit me all of a sudden, later on, that that was how the gun was got rid of. And sure enough, when I had Jerry take a swim in Hibler's boat slip, there it was, right on the bottom, where it had been all along."

Mollie Hammond came over to the desk and leaned and gave Dan a kiss on the cheek. "I don't care how you did it, Sheriff Peavy. I'm just glad you did."

She was mighty pretty when she smiled. I noticed, too, that she had done something to her hair, and she was wearing lipstick. Of course, Sam hadn't been dead long, but when a bit more time had passed, it would be perfectly proper for me to call on her.

Besides, Juanita and Thelma both might do well with a little competition.

NEVER MARRY A WITCH

C. B. Gilford

Tom Partain was a very devil with women. He was just natural-born to it. A talent like Tom had can lead to fortune—or to a peck of trouble. In Tom's case it was trouble.

Tom was tall, broad in the shoulders, lean in the belly, with strong arms and hands, the kind women like to be held and fondled by. He was handsome too, in a real masculine way, with straight, craggy lines to his face, and a tangle of light brown, unruly hair, some of which always came down over his brow above his left eye. Women figured that gave him a boyish look.

They flocked to his store. And why not? Women do most of the world's shopping, and the Partain Emporium sold just about everything. Some people wondered what had ever possessed Tom to become a mere storekeeper. There were two obvious reasons. One was that Tom's uncle had willed him the establishment, and a man does have to make a living. The other reason was almost as simple. What other business or profession gave a man the opportunity, six days a week, to have dealings with creatures of the opposite sex?

Tom did well. The ladies visited his store just as often as they could think of something to buy, and they stayed as long as they could. Sometimes there was a dozen or more of them in there at a time, vying to be waited on, asking questions about the merchandise, chattering, giggling, all striving for the proprietor's attention. There were other times too, when business was slacker, when the giggling might be heard coming from back in the storeroom.

There was really only one flaw in Tom Partain's otherwise idyllic existence. He had a wife. Her name was

Meg, she had property, and she wasn't bad looking. The day she took Tom to the preacher, some said, he had a strange, vacant look on his face. Drunk probably—he indulged sometimes. Or maybe hexed. Meg surely must have had some power over him to get him there. Anyway, that was what they said.

Meg was red-haired but self-controlled. She kept a loose leash on Tom. She knew about the dalliances down at the Emporium, but a certain amount of that, she also knew, was necessary for business. So, retaining legal ownership of Tom, she was content.

Till Audrey Mance came along. Well, she didn't exactly come along. She grew up. She'd been around town all the time, in and out of the Emporium, buying little things, maybe exchanging a shy word with Tom, a gawky girl who most probably had been fiercely in love with him for years. Then one day, like magic, like a fairy wand had been waved over her, she became a woman, with shiny black hair, eyes to match, flawless skin, and the cutest little figure Tom had ever seen.

Audrey wanted Tom; not just daytimes for pleasant raillery over a spool of thread; not just for kisses in the back room either. She wanted him, for herself, for keeps. And the way Tom looked at her, neglected other customers whenever she came in, everyone in town soon knew that trouble was brewing.

Everyone except Tom. Tom was blissfully ignorant. Because he loved women, he didn't understand them. He didn't, for instance, understand why he suddenly had a rat in his store.

Not rats, not an infestation, just a single, solitary rat; not a mere wandering rat, but one which seemed to know precisely where it was going. Tom was puzzled before he was worried. There was no food around the place; the Emporium didn't sell groceries. But the rat came anyway, boldly, in daylight, not like an ordinary rat at all. Even Tom sensed that this was a mighty strange thing for a rat to do.

It came in through some unsuspected crevice, sat in the middle of the floor, and stared at Tom. Tom stared back, too surprised to grab a broom or a gun, or do anything. Man and rodent stood looking at each other.

Tom was aware of a vaguely prickly sensation running up and down his spine—not quite fear, not quite wonderment. There was something unusual about this rat that wasn't just boldness. It went farther than that.

Maybe it was the rat's color—not gray, or black, or brown, or even white. Instead, the animal's fur was a kind of red that almost reminded Tom of . . . but that was a ridiculous notion!

They might have stood like that, staring at each other, almost forever, but the tinkling of the bell on the front door sent the rat scurrying. It was Mrs. Harrington, who took a shamelessly long time in buying a pair of shoes. All the while, Tom was mentally afraid the rat would put in another appearance, and Mrs. Harrington would run screaming from the store. If there was one thing the female sex couldn't endure, it was rats. One single rodent could ruin his business.

That presented a horrifying picture to Tom's mind. Most of his customers were women. If the word went around town there was a rat in the Emporium, not all of Tom's charms could lure the lovely creatures inside again. Business for Tom wasn't a business. It was a pleasure.

But Mrs. Harrington departed unscathed. Tom looked around. The rat was nowhere in view. *Forget it*, he told himself nervously, hopefully. The beast will go away when it discovers there's nothing to eat around the place.

At noon, when most of the town was having lunch, Audrey Mance slipped in. Tom had his back turned, didn't hear her enter, didn't even hear her as she ran lightly across the wooden floor, sneaked up behind him, raised herself on tiptoes, and playfully bit his right ear.

"Audrey," he began, "you shouldn't do that out in front here." For the moment, with sweet Audrey there, he just about did forget the rat.

"There's nobody around." She kissed him anyway.

It was a long, lingering kiss. When she withdrew her lips from his and looked up at him, her dark eyes were shining. "Oh, I love you, Tom," she said. "The way you put your strong arms around me, you just about crush the breath out of me; and the way your hands glide over my back, the way you kiss me, kiss me, kiss me—a girl doesn't have a chance at all."

Suddenly then, her expression changed. Her eyes stared, her mouth contorted. "There's a rat!" she screamed.

Tom glanced over his shoulder. There the thing was, high on a shelf behind him, its tiny black eyes glaring down at them, its tiny, sharp teeth bared in a snarl.

Tom reached for the glass paperweight on the counter, hurled it. His aim was accurate at that close range. The missile hit, and the rat squeaked in obvious pain and alarm. Then as both he and Audrey watched, fascinated, the animal ran the length of the shelf, limping, favoring its right front leg, till it found refuge somewhere in the middle of some bolts of yard goods.

Tom would have gotten the stepladder, chased it right then and there, tried to kill it with his bare hands, but Audrey was still screaming and sobbing. So, instead, he picked her up bodily, carried her to the rear room, and locked the door behind them, leaving the rat in possession of the store.

Audrey was quaking inside the protective circle of his arms. If there ever had been any doubt in Tom's mind about how females reacted to rats, there wasn't now. All the high color had drained out of Audrey's pretty face. Her eyes darted about in every direction like a madwoman's. "Where did that rat come from?" she asked in a terrified whisper.

"I don't know, I never had rats before."

"Please get rid of it."

"I will, I will. . . ."

"It's an awful thing. I'm scared!"

"Well, you really don't have to be." He covered her pale face with kisses. "Rats don't attack people."

He'd no sooner made that bald statement than he regretted it. What *could* a rat do, if it weren't frightened of human beings? That rat hadn't looked frightened.

"Forget the rat, I'll take care of it," Tom urged the girl. But she couldn't forget it, and the kissing wasn't very satisfactory that day in the back room.

"It's no ordinary rat," Audrey said after her tears

had dried a bit and she'd had some time to think the situation over. She was calmer, but her dark eyes were haunted.

"What do you mean by that?"

"It's witched, that's what it is."

That was a woman for you, and she wouldn't be talked out of it. She was scared clear through. He wanted to comfort her in the only way he knew how, but now she wouldn't let him touch her. He tried to interest her in a trinket, a scarf, a necklace, anything. She couldn't be distracted.

When she finally sneaked out the rear door, Tom was content to let her go. He returned to the front of the store and searched for the rat, gingerly moving things about on the shelves and peering into dark corners. He found nothing.

That evening Tom went home hopeful that the invader, injured and in pain, had vacated the premises for good. On the way he even stopped for a couple of pints of ale with his cronies. When he arrived at his cottage, he went looking for Meg to give her his dutiful kiss. That was when Tom Partain got the surprise of his young and eventful life.

"You hurt your hand!"

It was swathed in a white bandage—her right hand.

"What happened?" He was reaching for her, trying to get a good look at her injury, but she backed out of his grasp.

"Oh, it's nothing. . . ." She hesitated, but must have realized she had to explain in some way. "I was reaching into the fruit closet, and a glass jar fell down."

A glass jar—a glass paperweight!

"When did it happen?"

"I was getting something for my lunch."

About noon then! Audrey's regular time of visiting. It was all incredible to a practical man like Tom. He hadn't believed the rat was witched, but here was proof of even more than that. Meg could be—and was—in two places at the same time, in the body of a rat and in her own. He was married to a witch!

He rushed out to wash up for supper. All during the meal, he kept staring down at his plate, wondering if Meg knew what he was thinking. He had a red-haired rat in his store—it had seemed mighty upset when it saw him kissing Audrey Mance—it was really Meg who'd been upset so—and whatever you did to the rat, also happened to Meg—

From that point on, Tom's train of thought was riding on a very interesting track. He didn't want rats around his store, that was certain, whether they were plain rats or red-headed witch rats or whatever. One was as bad as any other, and he must get rid of it.

Beginning the next morning, Tom was a man with a mission. When he arrived at the store, the rat was nowhere in sight, nor did it put in an appearance later, but Tom was taking no chances.

The first and obvious thing to do was to set out poisoned food. Even a witched rat had to eat. Then he had his two weapons, a rifle and a shotgun, and these he set handily by, as well as such assorted items as brooms and broom handles, mops and mop handles. The final strategy was to borrow Fidelis, the McPhersons' big tomcat.

This last endeavor proved an utter failure. The moment he was brought into the store, Fidelis, a huge, fierce-looking black-and-gray specimen, arched his back and seemed ready to launch an immediate attack in the direction of the kitchen-ware counter. He even took several tentative steps, but then he appeared to catch a better whiff of his quarry. His fur rose, he quivered for a moment, then he let out a dreadful screech and leaped out the door, straight through the screen wire.

Tom Partain knew then what he was up against. No cat could ever catch his rat.

"But I've got to do something!" he said aloud.

He did the best he could. He set out the poisoned food, but it remained untouched. He watched endless hours for a sight of the rat, ready with his guns. He would willingly have blasted a shotgun hole in the side of his store, but he was given no opportunity. He saw nothing, he heard nothing. Yet he knew beyond any doubt that the vengeful rodent still lurked on the premises.

For a whole week Audrey stayed away from the Emporium. Tom was angry and lonesome, but he didn't try to seek her out at her own home. He wanted no scandal, for that would ruin his business as surely as the presence of a rat. So he tried to be patient.

Audrey finally summoned enough nerve to return on the following Monday. She knocked timidly at the rear door, and Tom, who had been half listening for the welcome sound, went immediately to let her in, first making sure to shut the door between the back room and the store proper.

The lovers rushed into each other's arms. "Oh, Tom," Audrey whispered, "I've missed you so."

"I've missed you," he answered, covering her face and neck with the kisses she wanted.

They were there together for quite some time. The tinkling bell on the front door was silent; no customers arrived to interrupt them.

"Have you gotten rid of it?" she asked finally.

"What?" He knew, of course.

"The rat."

"Well, I don't know," he lied, and she suspected that he did.

"Oh, Tom," she said, beginning to tremble anew, "you must get rid of it. You understand why, don't you?"

He shook his head stubbornly.

"It wants to bite me!"

"Now, Audrey . . ."

"Especially my face!"

Tom shook his head again, not wanting to believe such a horrible thing. "Why should anything want to bite that beautiful face of yours?"

"That's the reason, don't you see? It wants to ruin my face—tear my flesh to bloody ribbons with its sharp teeth—so you won't look at me ever again. Tom, your wife witched that rat, and sent it here, to watch us, to protect you, and to attack me!"

Tom understood only too well. It made sense. Meg

knew his weakness for pretty women, and only for pretty women. Meg was like that. She would want Audrey to be disfigured.

The other thing about the rat—that it wasn't just witched by Meg, but it was Meg—Tom did not offer to Audrey as a return of confidence. No sense in scaring her any more than she was already.

"You haven't killed it?" she pressed him.

"I've tried. I've tried my best. Poison, a cat, I've waited with my shotgun—maybe it's gone."

Audrey shook her head desperately. "No, it isn't gone. It's still here. It's looking at us right now, from some hiding place. I don't want my face ruined! I don't want to be bitten! We can never see each other again, Tom. . . ."

She screamed, as she had before, her features contracting with horror, her finger pointing. Tom turned in time to catch a mere glimpse of a small furry figure, slightly reddish, scurrying behind a barrel.

Tom lunged, ready to seize the thing with his bare hands. He thrust aside barrels and boxes, sent them crashing. But the rat was gone. He turned back, mad with frustration. "Audrey!"

But the rear door was ajar, and Audrey was gone.

Tom Partain was left facing his problem squarely. The rat was still there. It intended to stay. As long as it was there, he would be without Audrey.

For the first time, he really began thinking. High intelligence wasn't what women saw in Tom Partain. But now, sheer, desperate circumstances forced him to think clearly. He was appalled at what his cogitations turned up. He had been going about the business all wrong!

Now that his mind was clear, now that there was something that could be done, Tom became a man of action. There were no customers in the place, but if there had been he would have shoved them out. He shut and locked the rear door behind Audrey, then grabbed up a gunnysack and a length of rope from the storeroom, and walked up toward the front. At the door he paused a moment and glanced back.

The rat was there, he knew, somewhere amid the

jumble of counters, boxes, barrels, stacks, and shelves, moving about noiselessly, perhaps making itself at home. Or maybe just sitting still and watching him, even wondering—where he was off to at this time of day, what he was up to.

He smiled. *You'll see, old red rat,* he answered silently. *You just wait here a spell, and you'll see.* He put up the little sign in the glass front door announcing that the store was closed, walked out and locked the door behind him. Then he strolled down the main street of town, the sack slung over his shoulder. He turned right, cut across yards and fields, and finally plunged into the woods.

Now he was a hunter. He walked slowly, his eyes searching restlessly in every direction. The afternoon sun sank lower into the tree branches. But Tom was patient. He wanted a special thing, and he pursued it relentlessly.

He stopped suddenly. He smiled. Now he walked even more stealthily. Then he pounced. His prey struggled, fought against imprisonment in the gunnysack, but Tom won. Quickly, he tied the sack closed with the rope.

Tom took the long route home. Nobody saw him when he arrived back at the Emporium. It was dusk. He unlocked the door, slipped inside. He didn't need a light. He simply undid the knot in the rope, turned the sack upside down, and let its contents drop onto the floor. Quickly then, he made his escape, through the door again, locking it behind him.

He paused to smile, satisfied with himself. He listened at the door, but no sound came from within. The silence did not disturb him. He walked jauntily home to Meg.

She wasn't there. She was nowhere. The kitchen was absolutely empty of its occupant, owner and mistress.

To make absolutely sure, Tom searched the other rooms, poked around in the darkness of the yard. He called her again and again, softly, so neighbors wouldn't hear. But no answer came. Meg was gone. Vanished. As if . . .

"Yieee!" He could contain his elation and triumph no longer. Leaping, running, dancing, twirling, he sped away from the house and through the streets of the town toward his Emporium.

At its front door, so great was his excitement, he dropped the key half a dozen times before he could insert it into the lock. Inside, he hastily turned on a light. He blinked, stumbled around, till he almost fell over the thing for which he was looking.

Seven feet long it was, at least, and as big around as Tom's brawny forearm. Shiny black it was in the dim light. Lazily, torpidly, the snake raised its head and challenged him, the red forked tongue darting swiftly in and out. Satan himself had been such an inhabitant of the Garden of Eden, and now his descendant had been more than the equal of a "witched" rodent.

The monster's appearance had changed only slightly. In the middle of its long body was a swelling—not too large—just about the size of a rat.

Folks said around town that Meg Partain had just plain gotten tired of Tom's philandering, and one night had just up and left him. No one knew what had happened exactly, except Tom, and he could only imagine.

Of course, Tom acted bereaved at his loss. Soon, as folks watched, he began to recover from his sorrow and to court Audrey Mance openly. There was some legal business with lawyers, the outcome of which wasn't to declare Meg Partain dead, because there was no evidence of that, but rather to give Tom a divorce and his freedom. It was scandalous enough, even the way it was handled. But Tom was a nice fellow, and people were inclined to like him, so he was able to keep the Emporium open, and then one June day, to marry Audrey Mance.

But Tom really hadn't changed. His kind seldom do. Audrey stayed at home, happy to be his wife, but there was Tom, with all the women in town going in and out of his place all day. Eventually there had to be a special one.

Her name was Ellen Hardy, young, blonde and extremely shy. She fell in love with Tom like all the rest. She came in one day at noon, when the store was otherwise empty.

"Mr. Partain . . ."

"Hello there, Ellen."

"Mr. Partain, I've had my eye on that string of pearls for a long time. I wonder if I could try them on, see how they look."

"Why, sure thing. Here, let me put 'em on you. Ellen Hardy, you have the prettiest, softest, whitest neck I believe I've ever seen. . . ."

But as he bent to kiss that neck, the girl screamed. Her eyes were fastened in terror on a spot where, just emerging from between two hat boxes, was an enormous, shiny blacksnake.

"Ellen!"

But the girl was gone. Tom didn't follow her. Instead he looked at the snake, the fixed stare of its tiny eyes, the angry undulation of its gleaming coils.

"Audrey!" was all he said. Then he walked out of the store and never returned.

THE SECOND THIEF

David A. Heller

Nick Farrel considered himself a lucky man; a lucky man, indeed. It proved the truth of the old saying that it's worthwhile to make a play for every pretty girl you meet. Even if you only get a return of five percent on your investment, it's worthwhile.

Anna's slender arm clung possessively to his. Anna's blonde head rested dreamily against his shoulder. Anna's sweet, heady perfume was fragrant in his nostrils. Nick's fingers trembled as he fumbled with the key to unlock his apartment. He never thought she'd come.

How would she react? Would she be frightened? Anna was very young, not more than twenty. Anna's blonde hair was too flashy and her dress was too tight, too low-cut and too daring, but she did not look like the kind of a girl you picked up in a bar. He had known her less than an hour, and he *had* picked her up in his favorite nightclub, but beneath the flashy exterior, Nick could see that she was a girl of quality. Nick Farrel considered himself an authority on women with class.

Anna was not frightened, nor shy, nor too brassily bold. The red lips that had once been so haughty, but that had been coaxed to relax under his gay line of banter, now flashed into a smile and the icy cold had melted out of Anna's blue eyes.

"You didn't think I'd come, did you, Nick?" The words were a challenge, lightly mocking.

Anna's slender fingers squeezed Nick's hand with an electricity that sent tingles all through him, and he looked so startled that Anna laughed delightedly.

It was astonishing, really. Nick could not help

secretly congratulating himself upon his good luck. He had dropped into his favorite bar where he saw this dazzling blonde creature moodily sipping a martini and fending off masculine advances. He had caught her eye and smiled. Unexpectedly, she smiled back, and pretty soon she permitted him to buy her a drink. Two martinis later, Nick, as casually as he could, suggested that they go to his place for a drink. He almost fell off his stool when Anna looked him square in the eye and, reading his thoughts, knowing what was in his mind, the scarlet lips breaking into that wild, mocking laugh, she said yes.

It all puzzled him. In spite of everything, Anna did not look like the kind of a girl a man picked up casually in a bar.

Nick opened the door, snapped on the light, then closed the door behind them. Expertly, he tried to draw Anna into his arms but, just as expertly, she deftly eluded him and the flashing white teeth and the red lips broke into that alluring, mocking laugh.

"What's your hurry, Nick? Didn't you invite me for a drink?" Anna's blue eyes twinkled with an unspoken promise and Nick was encouraged rather than discouraged by the rebuff.

"Sure, honey. No hurry. We've got all night. Just make yourself comfortable." Nick felt very much the man of the world.

Confidently, he went to the bar that stood in one corner of his luxurious apartment and mixed two very dry, very potent martinis. A suave grin was on his confident face as he turned toward Anna. Then the grin faded. Anna's right hand held a tiny, but quite lethal-looking revolver, and it was pointed straight at his heart. Anna appeared nervous and that frightened him quite as much as the revolver. A nervous woman with a gun can make a deadly combination.

"Surprise party, Nick. I want the loot you stole in the Harrison Jewelry Company safecracking."

Nick was incredulous. So far as he knew, the Harrison job was one of his best. The police did not have a single clue to connect him with the robbery.

Cautiously, he risked a step toward the slender girl,

but she brandished the revolver and the wild blue eyes looked more nervous and frightened than ever.

"I'll use this, Nick, if I have to. Don't make me kill you. That would be too bad for both of us."

"How did you know about the Harrison job?" Nick demanded.

"Your M.O., Nick. You were too smart to leave any clues, but the police know your *modus operandi*. The Harrison job tagged you just as cleanly as if you'd left fingerprints all over the place. To an expert in safecracking, the Harrison job had Nick Farrel written all over it."

"What is this, the second-thief caper?"

"Yes, Nick. You've fallen for the oldest dodge in the underworld. Very careless for a smart thief like you."

No words had to be wasted talking about the second-thief operation—letting the first thief take all the risk and then robbing him of the loot. The first thief cannot, after all, go to the law for protection.

"You haven't sold the Harrison jewelry to a fence, so you have to have it. I want it. Now." Anna made a threatening gesture with the gun. "Don't stall, Nick. In a little while some friends will come up and work you over if they have to. You have a really good-looking face. It would be too bad to spoil it."

The thought of being worked over by a crew of strong-arm boys cooled any intention Nick might have had to resist. Reluctantly, as Anna covered him with the tiny revolver, Nick opened a hidden panel in his mahogany-covered wall, revealed a safe, and opened it in grim silence.

"Just the Harrison loot, Nick. You can leave the rest inside."

Nick gazed at the slender blonde in astonishment.

"Put the jewels on the table."

The sparkle of diamond rings, of ruby clips, emerald brooches and gold watches gleamed and glittered as the precious items spilled across the dark wood of the tabletop.

With a swift movement, Anna opened a brocaded party handbag. With her left hand, she removed a pair of handcuffs and tossed them to Nick Farrel.

"Put your right wrist in one side and lock the other to the arm of that sofa."

Nervously, but with obvious clever preparation, she directed him. "Quick!"

For an instant Nick's mind toyed with the idea of resisting, but the idea of a jittery woman with a gun sobered him. She could shoot him before he could reach her. It was annoying to be robbed, but better robbed than dead. There would always be other jobs. The Harrison job was typical. The police must have known it was he, but they couldn't prove it. They could never prove it.

Anna's blue eyes studied him. He was securely handcuffed to the heavy sofa.

"Have you ever thought of what your crimes do to people, Nick? Peter Harrison, the man whose store you robbed, was—or could have been—ruined by you. He was underinsured. A lot of people are careless about not carrying enough insurance, Nick, especially in the jewelry business. A wonderful old man could have been ruined by you."

Nick Farrel was in no mood for a lecture. "What difference does it make to you? You're a thief just as much as I am. Take the loot and get out."

Instead of leaving, Anna moved to the telephone and dialed a number.

"Police headquarters? This is a friend. There has been a robbery and an attempted murder at 1635 Meredith Avenue, apartment 5-C. You will find the loot from the Harrison Jewelry Company robbery there. Will you send a squad car right away, please?"

Calmly, Anna repeated the address, then hung up the telephone.

Turning to Nick, she said quietly: "You're a clever man, Nick. Quite good-looking, too, if it makes you feel any better."

Nick Farrel's reply was unprintable.

"When you get out, try your hand at something honest."

The wail of an approaching police car split the night. Nick Farrel listened in fascinated horror.

Only then did Anna leave—with the jewels still on

the table. She left the door to Nick's apartment wide open, and as the police were only seconds from entering the elevator door, Anna quietly slipped out the rear stairway.

As she scurried down the stairway, Anna Harrison, the daughter of Peter Harrison, who had almost been ruined by the clever thief, Nick Farrel, quietly slipped off the flashy blonde wig she wore. Putting it in her handbag, she fluffed out her natural dark hair.

No one was watching the back door, and Anna slipped through an alleyway and mingled with a crowd of people walking down Meredith Avenue. There were not many advantages to being engaged to a detective sergeant—when she and Detective Johnny Frazer were married, they would probably never have any money—but when Johnny had told her of his absolute conviction that Nick Farrel was the man who had robbed her father, it had planted the seed of the idea in her mind.

Now it was improbable that Nick Farrel would rob anybody else for a number of years; at last, the police would have the evidence on him.

THE NICE YOUNG MAN

Richard O. Lewis

The first three bars Freddie had visited that evening turned out to be sadly unrewarding. No one bought him a drink, and no one, either by word or deed, seemed to be aware of his very existence. Now, however, in the fourth bar, circumstances had taken a sudden turn for the better: *he had found a live one.*

The "live one" was in the form of a young man who had come in and gazed about as if looking for someone, and had finally taken a stool at the bar right next to Freddie.

"Join me in a drink?" he invited, smiling in friendly fashion.

"Scotch," Freddie said, pushing his half-emptied beer glass to one side.

The young man was dressed in slacks, sport coat, and turtleneck sweater. He wore a small moustache and a shock of blond hair that was too long to be classified as the young-exec look and yet not long enough to be rated strictly hippie. Freddie noted the expensive watch on the man's wrist, the billfold he had taken from an inner pocket of his coat, and the twenty-dollar bill he placed on the bar. He couldn't fit the young man into any definite category and didn't waste any time trying. The needs of the moment were too pressing to allow random speculation to interfere.

After finishing off two Scotches in rapid succession and finding a third one already waiting for him on the bar, Freddie gloried in his good fortune and, at the same time, became fearful that it might end all too soon. There was a desperate need to capture the young man's fancy in some manner, to hold his attention.

"You may not believe it by looking at me now,"

Freddie began hopefully, "but I—I was once on the stage. Had quite a following then."

"You were?"

Freddie nodded, elated by the young man's apparent interest. "Magic. Legerdemain." He became expansive. "Mundo the Magnificent, I was called."

"Well, well!" marveled the young man. "Just think of that!"

Freddie climbed down from his stool and drew himself up to his full height of five feet, seven inches. "You wouldn't believe the audiences I played to!" He held onto the bar with one hand while the other stroked the short gray beard that was as seedy and unkempt as the long, rumpled overcoat he wore. "I packed them in! Held them spellbound!"

"Wonderful," complimented the young man. "I'll bet you were a great success!"

Freddie's narrow shoulders suddenly sagged and a trace of moisture came to his bleary eyes. "Alas," he said, shaking his head slowly from side to side and climbing back upon his stool. "Alas, things have changed. There is no call for stage performances anymore, you know."

The young man nodded gravely, watched Freddie finish his drink, and ordered him another one. "Say," he said suddenly, as if a happy thought had just struck him, "I happen to be a magician myself. Not professional like you, of course—just sort of a hobby with me, something to amuse my friends. Perhaps you could help me smooth out some of my tricks and show me a few new ones."

"My right hand," said Freddie, holding it up. "Got it hurt a while back." He flexed his fingers stiffly. "Might be a bit awkward. . . ."

"Doesn't matter. You could show me in slow motion. And, of course, I'd expect to pay you for your trouble."

Freddie brightened, tossed off the drink he was holding, and gazed wistfully at the empty glass. "Maybe I could show you a few of the easier ones," he admitted.

"I'll tell you what," the young man said, glancing nervously at his watch, "I've got to meet a very important client right now, but it shouldn't take more than, say, forty-five minutes. I could pick you up at the corner afterward and we could go to my apartment."

"Right," said Freddie.

The young man summoned the bartender. "Give my friend another one," he ordered, "and I'll take a fifth of Scotch."

Freddie could scarcely believe that things were turning out so well. Maybe the siege of bad luck that had hounded him for the past few weeks was at last coming to an end.

"This might help to limber up the fingers," the young man said as the refilled glass and a packaged bottle arrived.

"Sure thing!" Freddie clutched the glass with one hand and reached doubtfully but hopefully for the bottle with the other.

"Not now." The young man got from his stool and tucked the bottle under his arm. "Later, when I meet you at the corner." He glanced at his watch again, and his fingers trembled slightly as he picked up some bills from the bar. "Buy yourself another drink or two while you're waiting," he said, indicating the two one-dollar bills and some small change he had left. "And remember, at the corner in exactly forty-five minutes."

"I'll be there," Freddie promised.

After the young man had gone, Freddie picked up the money and stowed it carefully away into a coat pocket. Then, glass in hand, he made his way to a small booth at the far side of the room. He turned quickly and focused his eyes on the large, illuminated clock behind the bar. Exactly ten o'clock. He sat down and began sipping his drink slowly and thoughtfully. He had no intention of spending the money in his pocket at the present moment. If the young man picked him up at the corner, there would be a whole bottle to work on. If the young man failed to keep his promise—well, he could use the money for a few beers at a cheaper joint and maybe finish off the evening with a bowl of hot soup.

After a while, he took some of the coins from his pocket, tucked them between his stiff fingers, made them appear and disappear, and plucked them out of thin air again. It was one of the very few tricks he knew, and his injured hand was not at all clever at it, but he felt he could bluff his way through for at least one evening.

As time dragged slowly on, Freddie found himself troubled by depressing thoughts. What if the young man had simply given him the brush-off? It had happened many times before, just when he had hoped things had changed for the better. Too many times! The feeling of depression brought with it the vague sense of loneliness he had so often experienced. What if, after forty-five minutes of waiting, he didn't . . .

He shook the thought from him. The fellow was just a nice young man, friendly, sympathetic and all. Probably a salesman of some kind—real estate or insurance—and had to see clients at odd hours of the day and night. Probably chose to meet him at the corner because he might have trouble finding a parking place for his car. No reason, really, why he wouldn't keep his promise.

When the hands on the clock behind the bar indicated ten-forty, Freddie drained the last drop of liquor from his glass, made a quick trip to the men's room, and then ambled out into the street. A chill fall wind had sprung up and there were only a few people about. He shoved his hands deep into the pockets of his coat and made his way slowly toward the corner. Finding no car waiting there, he shuffled over to a mailbox and leaned against it, depression taking hold of him once again. Perhaps he had let his hopes for a successful evening run too high, as he had done on several other occasions. He should have known better. Misfortune and disappointment had become a way of life with him lately.

What to do? Stand in the cold and wait for a young man who probably had no intention of showing up? Seek the warmth of another tavern and spend the rest of a fruitless evening drinking beer?

He was about to quit his post in utter defeat when a car slid to a sudden halt at the curb and a door flew open. Freddie pushed himself away from the mailbox, slid quickly into the front seat, and closed the door behind him.

"Had a bit of misfortune," the young man said, getting the car under way. "My client was sewed up with other matters—I'll have to see him later on. Here." He handed Freddie the bottle from the seat beside him.

Freddie wasted no time getting the bottle from its package, unscrewing its cap, and tilting it to his waiting lips. As the fiery, life-giving liquid trickled down his throat, his hopes for a satisfying evening began to soar again.

"Didn't want to keep you waiting," the young man continued. "A promise is a promise."

"Right," Freddie said. "A promise is a promise." He tilted the bottle again.

"The only thing I can do is to take you to my apartment and let you entertain yourself there for a while. This little business deal I have going for me happens to be extremely important, you know."

"Right," Freddie agreed.

The young man drew the car into a parking space a few minutes later and shut off the engine. "My apartment is just around the corner and down the street a ways," he said, getting out. "Can you make it all right?"

"Sure thing." Freddie got the door open, succeeded in getting to a firm standing position on the second try, shoved the bottle into the safe confines of a coat pocket, and followed the young man around the corner, weaving only slightly.

The side street was certainly not one of the better ones in town, definitely not the type of area in which Freddie had expected the young man to live. In fact, the street was not more than a dozen blocks from his own shabby haunts.

Halfway down the street, the young man turned suddenly into a doorway, and Freddie stumbled in after him. There were a few tin mailboxes along one wall and a narrow stairway leading upward. Freddie started up the stairway, pulling himself along with the aid of a railing that threatened momentarily to detach itself from the wall. Near the top, he missed a step, swung precariously back against the wall, and clung to the railing for dear life.

"Steady, old-timer," said the young man, clutching him under the arms and bolstering him up until he got his feet firmly planted again.

"I'll—I'll make it now," promised Freddie.

The young man opened the second door along the right side of the dimly lighted hallway, reached inside, and switched on the lights. Freddie surveyed the room with a quick glance. There was a closed door along one wall and an alcoved kitchenette in one corner. Although cheaply furnished, the room was clean and showed the unmistakable signs of a woman's personal touch.

"Not much of a place," apologized the young man. "But after I get this business deal under way, I'll be able to have something a lot nicer." He indicated the closed door. "We'll have to be fairly quiet—don't want to awaken the wife, you know."

"Sure thing." Freddie winked understandingly, took the bottle from his coat, and slumped down into an easy chair.

The young man glanced at his watch. "Hate to run off like this, but business is business. I'll be back in a half hour or so. Just some contracts and things to sign." At the door, he paused. "Make yourself comfortable. And remember, I'll pay you well for your time."

Once safely back in his car, the young man peeled the mustache from his lip, swept the blond wig from his head, and shoved them into the glove compartment. He drew in a deep breath and heaved a trembling sigh of relief as he got the car under way.

His affair with Millie had at first been merely a lark, a pleasing diversion, but thanks to her grasping nature, it had rapidly got completely out of hand. Her demands and threats had become intolerable.

"I want an apartment of my own, nice things to wear," she had insisted, "and no basement bargains."

"But I can't afford it."

"Then have your gracious and very rich wife increase your allowance!"

"I can't, and I'm already in debt."

"Then how would you like to have her find out about what you've been doing behind her back, and have her cut you off completely?"

Now, after finding the old derelict, and figuring out how to keep him waiting in the bar, he had been able to silence her threats and infernal bickering once and for all—and his timing had been perfect. Millie's roommate would arrive home from work within fifteen minutes or so. When she found the old drunk in the living room and discovered Millie's lifeless body on the bed, she would scream to high heaven, and the police would take it from there. Even if the old coot babbled something about a man with a moustache and blond hair, the description would lead nowhere.

Better for the old buzzard to be in jail than bumming about the streets for the rest of his life, he rationalized.

Left alone, Freddie waited until the sound of footsteps on the stairs had died away. Then he placed the bottle on a little table near his chair, pushed himself quickly to his feet, and walked softly to the closed door at the side of the room. He twisted the knob silently and pushed the door slightly open. Light stabbing into the room from behind him revealed a young woman sprawled out on the bed. She seemed to be sleeping quite soundly.

He pushed the door farther open and tiptoed to the bed. He looked at the woman's pale left hand. There was no diamond or wedding band there, just a cheap ring that could be picked up at any bargain counter—certainly not worth fooling with—and a quick survey of the room brought nothing of value to his attention.

Back in the living room, he fished a billfold from his pocket and opened it. A low whistle escaped his thin lips as the stiff fingers of his right hand fumbled through a goodly sheaf of currency.

Not too long ago, when Freddie had put his fingers

into another pocket, the owner of that pocket—a big man completely devoid of humor—discovered those fingers and twisted them unmercifully, putting a crimp into Freddie's means of livelihood. Even so, it had been an easy task for those experienced fingers to extract the billfold from the young man's inner pocket during the faked stumbling act on the stairway. It was the chance Freddie had been hoping for ever since he had spotted the billfold back at the bar.

He quickly jammed the billfold back into the safe confines of his coat pocket, picked up the bottle from the table and tucked it carefully under his arm.

At the doorway, he paused. The evening had been a great success, and since the young man had been such a nice fellow, buying him drinks and a bottle and offering to pay him for a few lessons in magic, there was no need to inconvenience him when it really wasn't necessary.

He took the billfold from his pocket again and extracted only the currency from it, leaving intact its contents of credit cards, driver's license, and other personal items—and tossed it into the doorway of the bedroom where the nice young man would be sure to find it when he came home later that night.

Under the circumstances, it seemed the decent thing to do.

A MESSAGE FOR AUNT LUCY

Arthur Porges

Five days after the Republic of West Africa closed its borders—"for reasons of National Security"—Dr. Neil Coburn was relieved to get a letter from his son, Kevin, obviously trapped in that hot-spot country at a critical moment in world affairs, with contact curtailed.

The boy, having just been graduated from high school, was spending a year abroad before going on to college, where he hoped to major in psychology.

Dr. Coburn and his wife were delighted to learn of Kevin's present safety, but they were greatly puzzled by the message itself. Either their son had not written it at all, a thought that made them wince, or he was suffering from some obscure tropical fever. Certainly the letter didn't read much like his normal style.

They discussed it at dinner that night. Some turns of the wording were unmistakably Kevin's, and yet there were comments that made no sense, if they understood their son's habits.

The doctor, his dessert untouched, read the letter aloud, as if hoping that the sound of his voice would remove the obscurities of Kevin's scrawl.

> Dear Mom and Dad:
>
> I've cajoled the officials here into letting me send this one note, an unusually kind action, since most tourists here are silenced until the borders reopen. But since I'm alone, and so young, they made an exception in my case.
>
> All I want to say is that I'm well, and treated with courtesy. This country is by no means as primitive as its detractors imply. The stores are remarkably well stocked. For example, I was even

able to buy a dozen bars of my favorite candy—
Almond-Pakt—which, as you know, I love to
gobble.

I do wish you'd show this note, bare as it is, to
Aunt Lucy, as I owe her several letters.

Much love,
Kevin

"It's all twisted," Dr. Coburn complained. "What's
the boy up to, anyway? That nonsense about candy,
for example?"

"I can't imagine," his wife said. "He'd just as soon
'gobble'—what a word!—arsenic."

"And that last part—dammit, Veda, he has no Aunt
Lucy. There was old Lucinda Barker, but she died
twenty years ago, before he was born."

"Aunt Lucy," Veda repeated thoughtfully. "Lucy,
Lucy . . ."

"No use chanting it," the doctor said in an irritable
voice, well aware he should be on his way to the hospital. "That won't help a bit."

She gave him a tender, but oddly cryptic stare, then
said, "For a brain surgeon, your own lacks imagination."

"Wha-a-at?"

"Kevin's a very bright boy, and there's no doubt he's
trying to tell us something."

"I figured that much," he said. "But what? Where is
the clue?"

"You never gave it a thought," she said calmly.
"Like all very competent specialists, you've a one-track
mind and almost no imagination. We've no Aunt Lucy
in the family—I wonder what Kevin would have done
if there were one—but don't you have a friend at the
British Embassy, Sir William Lucey?"

"Bill Lucey? Yes, but—why Kevin hardly knows
him. Why on earth would the boy make such a reference if he meant Bill?"

"I have no idea," Veda said sweetly, "but Lucey
might. After all, Kevin's always been up on interna-
tional affairs; he even knows all those new African

countries we can't tell apart. And isn't something brewing where he is? If not, why the closed borders?"

He blinked, was silent a moment, then said slowly, "Of course, you've hit on it. Kevin has something to tell Bill. I have to be at the hospital—overdue now—but you could take it to the Embassy. It may be important."

"I'll phone right away," she said.

Sir William Lucey, the bearer of a distinguished name, and a man of considerable value to his country, didn't look the part. He was small, round-shouldered, and had a bony, lumpy, asymmetric face that had only one expression: musing fish. But he had the Englishman's impeccable grooming, a beautifully modulated voice, and eyes that glittered with vitality and awareness.

He heard Mrs. Coburn out in silence, then read the letter. His expression didn't change, but she detected a hint of disappointment about his mouth.

"It suggests nothing to me," he said crisply. "But that's to be expected. Boy doesn't know me, nor I him. Has to come through you, I should think."

"Just what is the situation in that country?" she asked. "If I knew that—"

"Right," he said. "Here's the story, leaving out the frills. The Republic of West Africa is about to get off the neutrality fence. If she goes with the West, she'll get technicians from your country and maybe Israel, and start a big agricultural program. If she turns to the Communists, then East German experts will filter in—very secretly, I would guess—and set up rockets. Then, in a few weeks or even days, war with Rhodesia. That would put us all on the spot. England is damned if she helps Rhodesia, and damned if she doesn't. There are other angles, but the main thing is if we know *now* which way the Republic will jump, there are measures, through the U. N. and otherwise, that might prevent a bloody mess."

"I understand," she said.

"All right. Now then, what are the things about this

letter that don't quite fit in with what you know about the boy?"

"Well, the Aunt Lucy bit we can skip; that was meant to send us to you. Or is there some other angle, too?"

"I doubt it."

"Then there's really only one other discrepancy—the candy. Kevin's a pre-diabetic; he never eats large amounts of sugar. He has no favorite candy, and wouldn't think of gobbling several bars."

Sir William read the letter again.

"Almond-Pakt," he murmured. "Candy. Hm. Chocolate, I presume, with nuts—almonds. What the deuce—" Suddenly his eyes lit up. "I say," he demanded, "does Kevin speak any foreign languages?"

"He took German and French in high school."

"Almond-Pakt!" Lucey said, lips twitching. "Damned ingenious."

"What do you mean?"

"The French for a German is 'Allemand.' Almond-Pakt—Allemand packed—full of Germans! East Germans! The country has opted for the Reds—and war." Quite unexpectedly, he patted her hand. "But thanks to Kevin, we'll fox 'em yet." He ushered her to the door. "That's quite a lad. When he finishes college, maybe we can talk him into a Foreign Service career, eh?"

"His father wants him to be a doctor; you, a diplomat; I, a lawyer. But I know Kevin. He'll be—Kevin!"

Dell Bestsellers

F.W. WINTERBOTHAM
author of *The Ultra Secret*

THE NAZI CONNECTION

THE RIVETING TRUE ACCOUNT OF A MASTER SPY INSIDE HITLER'S REICH!

In 1934, British Intelligence Agent Frederick Winterbotham arrives in Germany to play his dangerous game. He dines with generals, drinks with Luftwaffe pilots, and befriends members of Germany's top brass. He has met the Fuhrer himself and is privy to Hitler's most secret plans. But will anyone in the complacent West believe the menacing truth of all he has seen and heard?

A Dell Book $2.50   (16197-5)